A. N. Irvano was born in California in 1990, and continues to live in the area. This is the author's third novel.

I0626160

With Kindness

By A.N.Irvano

Falling Horse Books

With Kindness

Copyright © 2014 A.N.Irvano

First Edition

Book Design: A.N. Irvano

This book is a work of fiction. Names, characters, business organizations, places, events, and incidents either are the product of the author's imagination or are used fictitiously. The author's use of names of actual persons (living or dead), historical events, businesses, places, and characters is incidental to the purposes of the plot, and is not intended to disparage any company, businesses, countries, or persons named or created in the work.

ISBN: 978-0-9960346-2-3

Library of Congress

Printed in the United States of America

"For women who are tied to the moon, love alone is not enough. We insist each day wrap it's knuckles through our heart strings and pull. The lows. The joy. The poetry. We dance at the edge of a cliff, you have fallen off. So it goes. You will climb up again.

"You rare girl, once again, you have a body that belongs to no lover, to no father, belongs to no one but you. Wear your sorrow like the lines on your palm. Like a shawl to keep you warm at night. Don't mourn the love that is lost to you now. It is a book of poems whose meters worked their way into your pulse. Even if it has slipped from your hands, it will stay in your body.

"You loved a man who treated you like absinthe, half poison and half god. He tried to sweeten you, to water you down. So you left. And now you have your heart all to yourself again. A heart like a stone cottage. Heart like a lover's diary. Hope like an ocean."

-Excerpt of a letter from Anaïs Nin
to Clementine von Radics

With Kindness
by A. N. Irvano

Chapter One

The weak bleat of a cow brought Lane to focus on her work. Though loud, the pule did nothing but remind her of the contrived efforts at hand as she took inventory of the breakfast danishes, then the cupcakes, and later the cookies. Lane looked over her work, dissatisfied with an err in numbers and twirled her pencil to erase and recalculate.

Again came the petition from the cow for any human hand to take a moment out of their day and lead it to a better place to graze. It had found a way onto the veranda, trapped close to the bakery's back egress and was swinging its neck left and right. Its call for help started off quiet, then gained to be rich in timbre before being cut off. It flicked its brown ears as the trembling sound of an explosion from the distance reached the open cloister. Lane looked up for a moment and the lines of middle age turned into panicked angles across her face before she breathed in and looked over at the cow. It gaped in longing towards a patch of virescent grass that sat nestled between roots of a mango tree and the smoky bricks of the cloister.

A coworker came into small office through the open doors of the bakery beyond and walked towards the archways to the calf saying to it, "Out with you!" before speaking with a more demure voice to the woman walking along the shadowed walkway under the cloister. "Oh, hello Harper!"

Lane noticed the woman's attenuate body enter through the pillars of the veranda's ingress. Her coworker bowed his head and went out of the office.

"Harper, I was beginning to wonder about you."

"Hello," came the pacifying resonance of Harper's voice. She patted the calf's head and walked onward past it and into the open-air office. With a clipped tone she asked, "Is work done, Lane?"

Lane mirrored Harper's curt fashion. "Nearly. What was that explosion I just heard? Anything to do with the agency?

"Yes, but not my department, Lane." Harper turned and felt for the cow's tether, then pulled herself and beast into the courtyard. Her head fell back while she watched the three drones, their black triangular forms moving noiselessly across the blue sky, and sighed.

Before they were out of sight she'd dropped her head and was searching the area around herself for a sufficient place to detain the cow. Without hesitation, she tied him to a cherry stained wooden pew and returned to lean against the tapered ingress, shielded from the sky by the veranda's cover. She idly watched Lane's emaciated umber hair brush the broadsheet that she worked above before her hands ceased operating to tuck it behind her ear and tighten the elastic band's hold on the bun.

Cognizant of attention upon her, Lane made soft sighing sounds and utterances as she appended the records to the final report, denoting an advancement in her tasks. With a low whine she closed the files and filed the paperwork.

"Now, my love," Harper declared as Lane turned from the work, "what is it we should do to quell that unease you have?"

Disconcerted at her temperance having shown, Lane's smile faded, only to return as she said, "I have a few ideas." Her eyes glittered as she swallowed her self-restraint. "Though none of them are very work-appropriate."

"Darling, you're off the clock." Harper sidled up to the window on the south side of the office. Moving her hands, Lane clutched Harper's legs and pulled them over her hips. She carried the woman out of the egress and into the cloister.

Upon their arrival a pair of doves made known their decampment from the innards of the mango tree with shrill mewls and flutterings of their wings. The calf remained immersed in its own chewing and the women sat entwined by the pew Harper had tied it to.

The reverberations from the three returning drones disunited the two as they journeyed out of the cloister. They passed under many pastel or neon painted ingresses and egresses, their curved shapes betraying the restoration efforts that had been undertaken after fortifying the shaken buildings. They took themselves ever further from the district Lane worked in until they were on footpaths where cement and asphalt did not dare broach.

The duo slowed when their ears alighted with a sound much like that of an approaching biplane. Soon, though, more bees had added themselves and they began to sound more like a group of children full of laughs, screams, incomprehensible word. The duo approached the hive and found themselves surrounded by something like the background noise of a short wave radio. Harper, being the more daring of the two, approached the beehive they paid a monthly fee to use. Her delicate hands slipped into the bright cadmium rubberized gloves that sat on a stand feet from the hive. She slid out one of the drawers and set it on the edge of the table, poking the propolis layers of each cubicle and then, tilting the drawer over a fresh jar from the stand, she let the blond molten food fall into the container.

She had slid the drawer back into the hive's cubicle. With an arresting stroke of her gloved hand, she decontaminated the ostensible areas of it and dropped it into her shoulder-bag. Besotted with Lane, she was glad to be able to join hands with her again, after removing the bulky gloves, and they walked on.

"Any air-strikes today?" Lane asked.

"Not in Sporat." Harper nodded solemnly as she spoke. "But in Kalcache and Jesup, yes."

"Casualties?" Lane asked as she twirled her body to sit under a palm tree. She unbridled her clothing and leaned against the trunk.

"Only a dozen because of the evacuation. The crafts were from Moscow." Harper did not sit. Instead, she stood with a straight back and eyes level with the horizon. This was her form of bereavement.

Off-handedly, Lane said, "They don't always seem to be from Moscow."

"We tracked the one in Jesup from an ally back to them, actually."

"Why do you think they're afraid to hit mainland with their own airliners?"

Harper was about to state her opinions, but the movement of the palm's leafy tendrils caught her discerning eye . She objectively thought of its movements and said, "I've been at the office all day; I really don't want to take it home."

Lane patted the sandy grass next to her and Harper sat. Lane removed the wedges off of her wife's feet. Harper sat in a reverie, watching Lane work at her feet. Her mind happened to filter out anything but the rumination on Lane's body as she moved about, picking up Harper's shins and setting them on her lap, then moving her hand up and down the abductor muscles of her thigh, as dark as a dried Mission fig and darker than any cursory time in the sun could ever produce on Lane's own body.

When Lane looked to her for validation, Harper jutted her black chin out, showing the gums of her bottom teeth and covered them with her plum lips, biting down. Lane kissed her jawline thrice before reaching her mouth and finding the inside quickly. They started a series of languorous kisses that de-escalated unhurriedly into inertness. For a quarter of an hour, the stasis prevailed and the two were wrapped in the arms of one another.

Chapter Two

Harper was again in her wedges, stamping them against the tiles of the executive offices as she remonstrated, "Reports! Informes! Ahora, now! Why not now?"

Her forty winks were over and the phrase, "Never the twain shall meet," was competing for attention in her gray matter as she felt the longing for the indolence she had shared with Lane during a time that remained in the past hours, wholly removed from the present moment.

"Lo sentimos mucho, I'm sure," Harper said as a staffer thrust himself into her office.

"Estoy," said the operative.

Harper shook her head as she opened the file. "You are?"

He shook his ead vigorously for her. "Trieste."

"Be sorry somewhere else," she said vehemently. There was bad news in the file. Her body slumped down to hold itself up no more. Her spine pressed against the plush brown leather of the chair and she held her natural hair in her hands, knowing full well that it would mold to the shape of her palms and look uneven and dismantled after this moment.

In this moment, though, she needed to cradle herself. Without any more irresoluteness, she grabbed her phone from her desk, sliding it and entering her password before opening it to the background of her and Lane.

She touched the corner of the screen and pulled on the phone to lengthen it into a larger tablet. She selected an icon and waited for it to open. When it did, she swiped her fingers along the screen and an icon of Lane's face was openeding and dialeding.

As she recognized her wife on the tablet's screen, Lane was said, "Heya!"

Harper sighed into her palm, letting signs of her bereavement register on the screen for Lane to see, saying, "Hey, pet."

"I didn't expect to hear from you this early." Harper watched the screen to see that Lane's eyes sparkled as her timbre wavered, like a pubescent boy's. "Is everything okay? Should I start us a dinner or should we just go out?"

Without being redundant, Harper said, "I'm going out of the country tonight." She let her head fall into her hands again and the globular black of her hair become all that Lane could see on her screen.

"That's okay, honey. There really is no problem with that." Lane cocked her head, wishing she could reach out a hand and pick up the face she'd seen falling. "You do all that you can, already. You do."

Harper was looking back up now, a smirk creating highlights of white dimples on her face and, looking at her own screen, Lane didn't know if Harper's cheeks were shiny from tears or natural oils. In any event, she made soft sounds of comfort to her and upended her eyebrows in apologetic concern for her wife.

Harper looked up, away from Lane, and shook her head, disturbed at who she saw. "Escapar, you!" Harper railed against the man at the door, who was there to collect the files back from her. Again, she spoke to him, "Salir," before walking over to the door and closing it, without a brief look at him.

"Will you come back tonight?" Lane asked with hesitation in her voice and a smile on her face when Harper returned to sit in front of her phone.

"You can count on it." Harper nodded, feeling the need to trace the outline of Lane's jaw against the touch screen of her tablet. Her smile widened, gratified to be able to act out the impulse to feel closer to Lane.

From the main room of the building Harper heard the resounding sound of a drill. Her eyes shifted worriedly, then refocused on Lane as she said tersely, "Got to go, now. Expect me around eighteen." She watched Lane nod as she swiped the call closed on the screen. She folded the phone into a loose cylinder and shoved it in her dress pocket.

A new man was at the door, speaking in a rush. "Do not collect your things, walk slowly and join the group to form a single file line."

"Real talk right now. I am running and I am taking my bags." She adjusted her clothing after throwing her purse and tech bag over opposing shoulders. "Thank you for your concern that I wouldn't join the cattle, though." The man's shoulders seemed to plummet as he watched her exit her office. He moved out of the way as she withdrew keys from her pocket and shook them expectantly. "I need to lock up." She shoved them through the keyhole, the ridges of it snapping into the places it knew well before being removed and put into the recesses of Harper's purse.

"Better join the herd," Harper said, jutting her jaw toward the throng of staffers exiting the building to stand, waiting for impossibilities in the cloister. Nodding, he sprinted toward them. Harper shook her head, dissatisfied with what she would have once considered inferior behavior, but today it was useful to her and for that she was obliged to hinder her vexation.

She clasped the silver-plated handle of her Oldsmobile in the parking lot, pulling stiffly and putting her bags in before she entered. Its low grumbles begged for disengagement but her feet pushed against its worn peddles, unmoved as it wheezed and importuned for retirement. Pedestrians walked across the streets alongside her car, no yearning to stay to their sidewalks but rather walking freely across the cracked and weary pavement of the roads. She drove heedfully, something that led to many people's bewilderment. So often she was enacted to do things that only she was comfortable doing, like becoming a vigilante of the road, that she rarely took passengers besides Lane.

"Hey, I know you're doing a lot right now, but I just found out the president has issued a new reform," Lane said to Harper when she arrived at their home.

Harper was an etched mask of intrigue, but concern leaked into her words as she asked, "What is it? Does it have to do with the hostile relations?"

Lane looked surprised to hear the strange alternative. "No, not at all. All electronic chargers are now mandated to be the same size and shape. No more having forty different chargers for everything." Lane had been more surprised and excited about what had seemed like an improvement, but Harper's supposition put it into the perspective of global crisis and it seemed much more meaningless now.

A tight smile was on Harper's lips. "That's great, but it's going to take awhile for everything in Cuba to convert."

Lane was simply regurgitating the news now. "The reform is countrywide and special measures will be taken to ensure the alleviation of all citizens' qualms in the matter."

"You don't really believe what you're saying, pet?"

"Not after you contrast it with hostile relations, no."

"Good, I don't want to leave knowing you lost your marbles."

"Harper," Lane began and her wife had her eyes on her quickly. "It's not getting better, is it? I know you can't say much, but I can tell, just from watching the news."

Harper sighed, pretending to be distracted by twirling her short black hair, and asked her, "What does the news tell you?"

"They'll bring up big crisis after big crisis and then without ever talking about the resolution to those, they'll bring up an itty-bitty thing like this and pretend that it's been solved when that isn't the problem," Lane said.

"You know what the Krussians used to do?" Harper leaned her head over to Lane's.

"What would they do?" she asked back.

"When there was something really terrible that happened within their borders, the media reported on something that had happened somewhere else, to get the citizens' minds off of the internal problems. It got to the point that when some Krussians—smart Krussians—heard reports of disasters in foreign countries, they would call their friends outside of Krussia to hear about what had happened in Krussia."

"They're land hungry. They have all of the power a country could want, but they want land, right?" Lane asked.

"It's much more complicated than that." Harper tilted her jaw away from Lane and stroked it idly.

"Hostile relations are the real problem. An impending world war is the problem."

Harper draped her arms over Lane's shoulder and she began swaying her hips. "We've been in an impending World War for decades with Krussia, I don't think you are going to change that much of it by being angry about it.

Lane turned her body away and said, "You slight me with your under-estimation, Harper."

"You are so cute when you're worried."

"Don't marginalize my concerns," Lane protested as Harper's hands wrapped around her waist.

They shuffled around the floor, dancing slowly. Lane's head fell to Harper's shoulder, steadied by Harper's hand on her hair. She stroked it playfully, knowing she wouldn't have the opportunity to touch tendrils of hair like hers for days, and so she treasured it now.

"No fresh food," Lane muttered.

"That's no good," Harper said. "Let's go to the plot?"

Lane smiled, giving a soft, "Mhmm."

Harper changed shoes and Lane grabbed a well-used bag and they trotted out the back door, past the porch and behind their garden to a long trail with no foliage coverage. They held hands on their walk and Lane leaned against Harper again, letting her be mindful of their stride for the both of them. When they got to the large community garden plot area, they found the cherry tomatoes on the vines near the entrance were ripe and Lane ran back to a basil plant they had found to pick from it.

"Mint water tonight," Harper called to Lane. Obedient, Lane bounded toward the mint that covered a table-sized patch of ground and bundled some up. They walked back and cooked a dinner together before Harper received a message and got into a black SUV, destined for the airport. Lane waved and stood in their home's entrance for moments, counting the feelings that passed through her before feeling contented to be alone. Only then did she return inside.

Chapter Three

"Briefing?" Harper asked in the car.

The driver said, "You know that you don't need one."

Harper ground her molars together and said, "I need one."

He told her, "Don't mess it up, Madame."

"Don't call me that, and tell me what I'm supposed to do this time," Harper spat back to the driver. She knew the man driving was technically her subordinate, but the entire idea of her as supervisor in Cuba was a farce made to appease her. Only allowing herself to have a slight awareness of her irrelevance, though, she chose to mask this fact from even herself to make the idea of her position in the agency plausible.

"Kill them with kindness, ma'am."

Harper replied, "You're not briefing me on what to do this time?"

"Oh, you'll know what to do."

"I don't know about that, what with your gross lack of reportage on what I'm about to take on."

He laughed snidely, then, with a voice like glass shards underfoot, he asked, "You can still take it, can't you?" Harper grabbed her dark brown arms and looked at the pink skin of her fingers against it. She shifted uncomfortably in the back seat and she saw that the agent's eyes watch her do this.

"Yes," she said vehemently.

"Where?" he asked.

She groaned audibly. "You disgust me, you know. So I'll be doing the old routine?"

His voice regained neutrality and he told her, "That will be all that is needed."

"Is the target already aware of me?" she asked, her voice diligent while her heart fluttered in an odd, anticipatory way. She never could quell her fear of rejection.

"You bet. Likes the look of you."

She thought she had a very good idea as to the answer, but asked, "Who is he?"

The driver just laughed.

She looked out the window, finding no resolve in the conversation. She said, "You're being awfully curt with your description of the target."

"Sensitive information," came the reply and she knew the conversation was over. She looked out the window of the car the same way she looked out the window of a plane. She picked at her hair with her fingers and sculpted it like clay to make her skull shape more prominent. She did small exercises in her seat and sucked her cheeks in and out to work on defining her cheekbones. Even the smallest things helped.

Chapter Four

Down in the 52nd state of America, Lane was waking up as Harper's plane pushed through the skies to land along the precursory runway. Before she could board the next plane, though, she was handed passports and identifications in Washington. They only resembled her in picture, not name or nationality. She handed off her actual identifications and was boarding another twin-jet by the time Lane was done tallying up sales reports and sitting in the courtyard behind the bakery.

Lane looked to the sky, seeing no drones flying today, and obliged herself to allow for an hour of quietly observing the scene. The mango tree's ashen, delicately thin trunk extended and then abruptly splayed out into branches and clusters of leaves. Their waxy leaves were characteristically oblong, elongated in the same shape as the Bowen mangos that swung from the spindly fingered clutches of the tree. Congregated but not ripe, the red and greens of the fruit were muted behind the veil of leaves from which they stemmed. Not yet tender and still displaying all of their colors, the tricoloured fruit resembled a stop light, hanging from green wires and stained with the carmine, cadmium, and emerald of the streetlight's burning orbs. Only when the breeze swayed and the shiny oval leaves allowed brief glimpses of all that they hid was the tree's full prosperity made obvious.

The dapple lighting from the tall mango tree played across the gray bricks of the courtyard, which held the desiccated and once gelatinous innards of the mangoes from years past in the cracks between stones.

Lane looked at the tree's leaves, remembering a time when she did not know trees had individual leaves. Before she had contacts, she had thought trees were large masses of green, but now that she knew there was singularity in the leaves she didn't know how she could have conceptualized a tree as anything but a collection of small, individual leaves. She set to finding the patterns in the way they grew and hung, dimples twitching wide as she gazed upwards.

Chickens and cows ambled in and out around her and she watched them both with a smile. Inside of her was a small fear that she listened to too often, that Harper would not come back. Invested in the fear fully, she let herself enjoy things for both herself and for Harper, as if she were dead and her smile would never grace the earth again. After letting that feeling linger in her for moments on end, she felt a need to leave the area, hoping it would dispel the mood.

At home, she watched the newest film, a remake from an old book she had never heard of before. She watched as the Don Quixote character, a stunning actor from mainland America, wooed and swayed an actress she had recently seen portraying a lesbian in another film. Lane watched, nervously anticipating her desires for their relationship to blossom and form. Morally, she felt opposed to her own anticipations, hoping instead that the woman would keep her pride and persevere against Don Quixote. Physiologically, though, she hoped to see them touch tonsils.

She vaulted from the couch when they did, white wind-powered energy mills swaying in the background and his little jokester companion jumping up and down nearby. She shook her fists in the air in celebration and sighed as the credits rolled. Nothing interrupted her afternoon and she took a quick glance at the news, but she succumbed to criticizing the advertisements instead of reading the articles.

Deciding to do something useful, she packed her karate uniform into her gym bag and revved up the Oldsmobile. She drove slowly, knowing she had time to spare before the nightly class, and filled up the tank, using the biometric payment system with a slight fear of lacking funds. Her hand twitched while the processor scanned the veins in her palm and fingers and found her account. She always considered that she wouldn't have enough, coming from a long line of entry-level workers. Harper's government funds allowed her to live well, though, and she bought a wrapped sandwich for after the class.

In the dojo, after warm-up exercises, they practiced upper blocks and Lane saw herself in the mirror before her arm raised or lowered to block her vision. She followed along with the Japanese numbers, seeing herself and then not. A smile twitched onto her face and she saw it in the mirror as she thought how it looked like she was blinking rapidly.

"Middle blocks! Hajime!" yelled the sensei and a focused line replaced her smile as her arms lowered.

"Now," began the instructor as he nodded to the class. They all sat down and he continued, "when you are switching your arms, they should cross in front of you, like a medical cross. Who has seen the American Red Cross?" The twenty hands in the class flew up and Lane noticed her attention increasing as he said, "I want you to think of that when you are doing your middle blocks. You are making a cross in front of yourself, protecting your body, like the Red Cross does. Understand?"

The class nodded and he lifted his hand, lifting his students with the motion. "Hajime. Lane, count."

"Ichi," she began with solid strength permeating in her voice, "ni, san, shichi." Tthe sensei stood between the mirror and herself, making the block motion with her count., "Hachi, kyui, juoi." He called out another student's name and they began counting into the twenties, adding the prefix ni- to the numbers Lane had said. The sensei reached out a hand and Lane inhaled as he grabbed and moved her arms with her. She kept moving, eyes darting back and forth between him and her arms. He nodded, unsmiling, and moved on, holding his hands behind his back as he counted for the class into the thirties.

The rest of the class went slowly as the sensei had them sit on their feet and shins and listen to him speak about the relationship of self-control and quick reflexes. It was often difficult to make the assertion of which to rely on, but experience was what would help them most. His lecture devolved into promoting his next training class that the monthly fees did not cover. He hid behind the thin veil of Japanese culture and its place in the lives of Americans and Cubans alike in order to make a profit.

Some of the class did not understand English and he would insert Spanish words into his rhetoric, smiling and laughing to himself as he did. Lane wondered how self-aware he was, but found herself thinking with an air of self-assuredness she had not gained the right to reserve.

In her car, parked against a cliff, it concerned her that she could look at a large storm forming around her and think that she had suffered worse and would face no problem getting through it. She could be steadfast and strong-willed in actual thunderstorms; as waterlogged as she may be, she would always return home.

Though, when there was trouble on the horizon of her life she would quiver and shake, knowing she had already suffered worse and thinking she couldn't go through any more of the same.

She thought how love could move in on her like a cloud bank, ready to be pushed by the hills and crests of her heart and soul or to wrap in the valleys of her mind, but she remembered this: it would seem to leave for a number of seasons, but ill weather always returns.

She bit into the sandwich, allowing it no mercy as she pushed it in with both hands and moved her head up and down and side to side as she ravished it. The condiments dripped out and accumulated around the creases of her lips and she allowed only a moment of separation from it to smile while still chewing, looking endearingly at it before she put it back in her mouth.

Chapter Five

A stewardess asked Harper, "Vegetarian or meat entree?"

Harper waved a hand, saying nothing, forcing the stewardess to walk past the aisle and leave her be. Harper had been given separately itemized amounts of food, all of which would prevent bloating or gas, unlike the in-flight meal that had been offered. She touched the terry cloth blanket absently, watching the actors on the screen on the backside of the headrest deal with their pointless problems in inexplicably dumb ways.

"I love this one," came the gruff voice of the man next to her.

Harper had been having trouble engaging in the movie and the interjection did not help. She scoffed, "Really? I find it trite."

"This one reminds me of Chaplin," he said and she gave a roll of the eyes. "You're too young to know a thing about him, though."

"Chaplin?" she asked. He smiled smugly and she told herself she was simply taciturn and didn't feel like responding. The movie did not take hold of her eyes and she found herself giving side-long glances at the man. She couldn't take the way his smile stayed pasted to his face in a self-satisfied way.

"Chaplin helped an almost pacifistic public think while entertaining them," she began, heavily forcing the words onto his person, "and he posed a threat to the government because he could inform the uninformed on the reality of the situation they were surrounded by. I know about Chaplin, sir. Do you know about him?"

The man gaped his mouth and he reminded Lane of so many other stooped, ghostly men whose behaviors were beyond the pale. She did what she knew best to do to them: she berated him until he fell to his knees for her. "He was logically secular but did not reject Jesus by agreeing with many of his teachings. Chaplin comparatively spoke on topics of greed, happiness, and love and his arguments are not inconsistent with the Bible's teachings. Chaplin was on a fight to free the world and his characters paralleled the struggles many Western cultures were facing, as well as the character of the Shakespearean fool, which was free to recognize and openly make illogical and misguided thoughts. I know

Chaplin. This movie, this smut, does not echo Chaplin." She pointed to the screens. "Unless you count the quirky way that one guy carries on."

The man slunk deeply into his seat before saying, "You got a mouth on you, don't you."

"You're the one that opened yours first."

"That I did, Miss."

Harper's diverted her eyes back to the screen.

Leaning over her, the stewardess placed the man's meal on his tray and clasped her hands, cocking her head, "Anything to drink for you?"

Harper lowered her voice. "Do you have a sleeping mask?"

At the cessation of the plane flight, Harper was nodding curtly to the antediluvian man she had talked to. She began to step down the stairs, surveying the airstrip. Normal baggage cars were parked around the plane as well as a nondescript black sports utility vehicle. She looked away, seemingly unconcerned. She walked all of the way down the ramp.

On the ground, she found herself approached by a man of the country her feet were on. She let her chin fall to her shoulder and lifted an arm, waving each finger delicately at him as he laid eyes on her and stepped towards her purposefully. She scooped her purse closer to her body, thankful she only had a carry-on and nothing that needed picking up from baggage claim.

"Hello Miss," he said with a heavy accent, tilting his sunglasses down and standing at the ready, legs apart and hands clasped above his groin. "I am Nikolav."

With an accent of her own, she said, "Hello to you. Are you the—"

"No, no." She wanted him to think nothing imposing about her and was thankful he cut her off.

She twisted her shoulders. "Well, should I follow you or something?"

His shoulders tightened as he nodded and turned, walking her to the SUV. He held the door for her and she got in, finding herself refreshed by the outside air and stretching her legs on her suspended walk from the plane to the car. The driver and Nikolav held halted, conventional conversations in Krussian that Harper listened to carefully. She found they knew their route well and would discuss the possible impediments before they were actual issues. They drove well and fast and only after a half-hour did they start to talk candidly about their personal problems and opinions of her.

"Very black," she heard and, in case they were watching her, she kept a smile on her face.

"I didn't know he liked that color."

"He does. She is skinny. It makes up for it, to me."

"Too skinny. What a small chest."

"Our Krussian women do not have such a problem."

"Unless they're dancers, no, definitely not." After that, the talk about her came to an end and she was happy for it.

She was beginning to betray emotion, tapping her fingers against the doorframe and looking around.

To make herself laugh, she wondered if they had ever played the I-spy game with their own race by walking into a room and seeing if there were any people in it that were the same color as themselves. She had played it often, not always feeling like she was part of a group, but merely the token in it. White people often forgot that racism was still a problem and poked fun at people of color. Harper liked to poke back and see if she could play her game while they played theirs.

"Almost there?" she asked in a high timbre. She stretched her neck to make it seem she was looking out the front window, but really she was checking to see where they had put their assault weapons. It was force of habit.

Nikolav made a brusque noise at her and quickly told the driver, "She's getting impatient."

"Tell her she has a lot of waiting to do," came the driver's response.

"Not too long now, Miss," Nikolav said in English.

She smiled obligingly. "Oh, good. Can we go somewhere to eat? I'm very hungry."

"No."

She began tapping her fingers against her inner wrist. She let her eyes roam over the bulbous tops of the outmoded buildings. Fleetingly, tall rectangles grew from the ground, erected by generations past and uninhabited by generations to come. Without allow it to infest her mind, she felt a longing for Lane's face. Seeing her own opaque reflection in the car's window, she knew Lane wanted to see her, too. To be able to call her and see her face on her phone's screen would have been enough, she thought. Without a second thought about it, she willed the thought to disinhibit her mind and she eyed both men speculatively.

The rarity and paradoxes of mysticism were what made it sound deep and truthful, which was usually enough to make Harper cast anything like mind-reading as a non-concern. But today, for the first time, in the SUV, she worried that the men could read her mind and would know her intentions were not true. Then again, she told herself, there are probably plenty of lesbian prostitutes. If the most they think about me is that I miss a woman's touch, I'm in the clear. She had had years of experience pretending to be paid for sex with rich white men. This time was no different. Given, she had not been to Cuba in some time. If anything, sex with only Lane had made her tighter, more desirable. Here's to hoping he doesn't have a chance to get in there. She smiled as she thought to herself, Okay, that's enough, Harper.

"Are you sure I can't get a burger or something?" she asked in a whiny voice that did not suit her.

Nikolav spoke in Krussian with the driver and he nodded curtly. Harper smiled and they turned off of the road onto another one. They passed an underpass besotted with hobo camps and a length away stopped outside of a McBurger's;, the company was an American transplant.

"You took me here?"

Nikolav shrugged. She stepped out and walked to the entrance. The line moved fast, too fast for her liking, and when she got to the register she asked, "What does the chef recommend?"

In accented English she got a reply. "Ma'am, this is a McBurger's."

"You're right," she said. "I'll have the cheeseburger. The big one. The one with three on top of one another."

"Three cheeseburgers?"

Harper shook her head. "No, just one with the mass of three. Isn't that something you have here?"

"No, ma'am," came the reply with a steady smile.

Harper smiled grimly. "Just three cheeseburgers then, thank you."

Chapter Six

When Harper had landed in Krussia, Lane was waking up and walking to work in the early light and dry morning in Cuba.

"What are you doing tonight?" asked Lane's coworker.

She shrugged her shoulders., "I'm not going out, I know that much."

"Oh," he tilted his shoulders as his voice fell. They tied the ribbons around the packets of cookies. It was the last step and the two were cheerful to be done with a task, though they knew there would be a new one coming up for them afterwards.

"Hey," Lane said to a customer as she moved over the register and placed her hands on the tablet. "What can I get you?"

The woman was nice and friendly, but she was rushed and gave Lane reason to shake her head after she had watched the woman impatiently press her palm to the thermal imager. The biometric payment system usually scanned the warm blood pumping through the hand—a labyrinth more individual than a thumbprint—quite well, but the woman had lifted her hand too quickly and it couldn't find her account.

"Try again," Lane offered. Lane waited patiently while the woman muttered as she obliged. "All set," she said with a smile when the tablet had verified the thermal image. The woman rushed out, nearly forgetting her bag of sweets.

"What about you?" Lane asked her coworker.

"I was going to go out for drinks, but I don't know now if you want to go."

Lane smiled, knowing it would become an argument in a week when she explained it to Harper. "Thanks, but no thanks. Other than that, how are your studies going?"

"Busywork, just like this, constant busywork. But I am writing an interesting essay."

"That's like saying you know you're beautiful." She gave a laugh as a sign of good nature and asked, inquisitively, "What's it about?"

He explained the premise to her as he placed cupcakes into their tiny boxes, "How people would grow and learn on a different planet, like Mars, assuming all of the right conditions for life were met. "

"Sounds interesting. What inspired you?" she asked.

He shuffled his hands in front of him and stopped working to talk. "There may be a time in our lives when we're able to know there actually are people living on Mars. We don't know what that feeling would be like, if we would feel differently there, if we would live longer. You know, there are so many possibilities. But we do know what it feels like to be bound to Earth. We also know what it feels like to be in different classes and bound to those."

She asked, "Like schools or a caste system?"

"Caste," he said. "You know that in America you are bound to whatever class you were born into."

"Or marry into," Lane appended. "It's arguable, but go on."

"Well, imagine what the class system would be like on Mars. Here you are on this new, limitless place full of possibility and you're held back by the systems that have always held people back. Depressing," he said, hastily shaking out the butcher paper he was working with and avoiding eye contact with Lane.

"So you're saying there would still be reason for sadness there?"

"Imagine the possibilities for the range of emotions. It would be totally different."

"That's like saying that our sun makes a specific array of light and, therefore, a different galaxy has the potential to have different visible light spectrums."

"That goes against what I know of astrophysics," he said. "I want to be prepared for that time, though. You know, disillusion myself before other people do it for me."

"I do like the premise of your essay. What class is that for?"

He told her, "Evolutionary philosophy."

Lane nodded and cocked her head as she focused on the ribbon-tying and her words at once. "There used to be a time when people believed in the future being so bright and shiny."

"Now we look around and see people that don't believe in that near and distant scientific future taking hold, but that future is coming."

"I think it'll look a lot like this present moment," she said, "dingy like it."

He said, "I definitely want to explore how people would feel in a dirty and sad future, not a bright and shiny one."

"Explore them both."

Lane finished work hours later and left through the front door. She sprinted back to her home, hastening her journey with a shortcut. She threw her yoga mat into the Oldsmobile and took the scenic route to the yoga studio. When she was there, she rolled out a yoga mat over the blond wood floor. The smell of sweat that was entering her nose was both familiar and disgusting to her and, like smelling gasoline, she both detested and was dependent on having it.

"There's a bucket of coins," began the instructor, "at the back of the room. What I want you to do is grab one of those coins and put it in front of your mat if you are okay with me, the instructor, touching you in order to provide assistance in your yoga form and practice. Namaste." Lane looked back and forth to the instructor and bowl.

She was in the middle of a salutation stretch. She pushed one ankle from the ground to point to the sky, in a scorpion pose, then brought it down below her belly and chest, and brought her body back to the ground, stretching over her bent leg, in a warrior posture. She looked, again, to the bowl of coins. They were wooden and had lotus insignias on them, but Lane could not see them that closely as she was still sitting on her mat in the center of the room.

"Let's start," the instructor said, clapping his hands and setting the lights low. He was pushing play on the music as she glanced once more to the bowl, her face full of resignation as she brought her body into the lotus position.

The doorbell rang twice the following day. The doorbell in Harper's and Lane's home, where only Lane lay. She smiled, remembering the doorbell ringing when she was a kid and running to the door to see who it was.

Now, she just ran as far from the door as she could and hid. She was mildly curious as to who was ringing, but it was a very nervous, stressed anxiety that made her breathe heavily and lay flat under the blankets she had piled over herself. After holding herself in a fetal position and rocking to and fro, she removed herself from the mass of blankets.

She sat at the table and held a to-do list in her hands. She liked the feeling of the graphite and clay pencils she had used as a child, but these were apparently smoother and glided from thoughts to words like a hydrofoil boat in shallow gunkholes. She wondered what had incited the change and something in her thought of the pre-wartime efforts of the nineteen hundreds spent rationing pencils and paper.

She thought she was setting out to make a to-do list, but she wrote nothing but what was on her mind and it quickly became something like a love letter.

Harper,

Our bodies.

Our bodies pressed.

Our bodies pressed together.

Our bodies pressed together combining.

Our bodies pressed together combining something.

Something spectacular.

Something spectacular that only we know.

Something spectacular that only we have.

And yet, it is something that we share with the rest of the world.

Something spectacular. Who has not done this?

We have all done this.

Miss you,

Love you,

Lane

After, she bobbed the pencil between her lips then set it down, leaving both pencil and pad of lists on the dining table. She didn't use the table when Harper was gone and it would not be moved.

Lane poured herself some of the mint water she had made with Harper and thought how she was so absent, so apathetic, when Harper wasn't around. She hadn't gone to any of the community plots in the last two days and didn't plan on going to one until Harper got back. Even though they were accessible to every individual, she felt like they were closed to her if she wasn't sharing their abundance with another.

Gathering her motivation in the look she gave the clock, she decided not to do anything before work, so she sat down to watch projections in the living room. The T.V. opened to recommendations and she chose to watch a film that featured the same actress she had seen in Don Quixote before going to work at the bakery.

"What are you doing?" asked Lane's coworker.

"See that man? He's been wondering if that man across the room likes him."

"How can you tell?"

Lane smiled. "I can tell."

Her coworker followed the agitated movements of the man she had first pointed out.

She aimed her eyes at him. "See how he looks up, then away when the other guy looks towards him?"

"Yeah I do," he said.

"Oh, oh!" Lane grabbed her arms and jumped up as the first man raised himself from his seat and, with a set look of determination, walked towards the other man. Both bakery workers were breathless as they watched. He stood next to the man and coughed, holding his body awkwardly over him.

"Finally!" said the seated man. Lane inhaled sharply, smiling into her balled-up fist. "I've been waiting to make an order for half an hour!"

"Oh," groaned both Lane and her coworker.

"No way," Lane said, tears springing to her eyes as her jaw dropped.

"What...do you mean?" blubbered the first man.

"Oh, you're not a waiter?" asked the man. He seemed slightly embarrassed now, then said, "you're dressed like one."

Lane set her jaw and walked forward from behind the register to the men. "Sir," she said the customer, "you need to order at the register. This isn't some ritzy mainland place that serves lazy junk to lazy customers. Now, if you're not going to reciprocate the attention this man was giving you, I have the right to refuse servicing you."

"Let's talk about the incident today," said Lane's manager later that day, in the office.

"I was doing what I thought was right," Lane attested.

Her manager said quickly, "I know you were, but was it really right?"

Lane nodded. "Yes."

"What are some different ways you could have handled the situation?" her manager asked Lane.

"Poured water in his lap," she offered, "while singing a lullaby."

"Lane, if I wasn't indebted to your wife I would have half a mind to fire you for that incident," her manager told her harshly, leaning back in the chair and away from Lane.

Lane felt her left eyelid twitch as she sat there. An involuntary reaction of her body meant that she was losing control of herself in more ways than one. Her eye twitching could be a larger sign of health problems. She could have inflammation of the cornea, a brain tumor, or a vitamin deficiency. The fear of health problems reminded her that there were more important things than an entry-level job.

She was thinking that there were more important things than this job, and yet, she wasn't able to do well at it. Her mind quickly began discerning her worries as she thought, If I can't do well at the simplest of things in life like this job, how can I reasonably be expected to take care of the larger things, like vitamin intake and the impending decisions related to a possible brain tumor associated with my eye twitch?

The realization made tears spring to her eyes. She didn't want her manager to see, so she ducked her head down and nodded apologetically.

"I'm going to give you a moment, but I want you to know that there won't be any free rides after today."

Lane tucked her mouth into a smile and looked up, nodding. "Thank you."

"You've been warned," her manager said, shocking Lane into holding her face in the palm of her hand as she tried to remind herself of the things that were more impactful than a job like this one.

She worried that she was biting her tongue. When she bit her tongue and was then asked to voice what she thought, she found more often than not blood came out rather than words.

She didn't want that, but she didn't want to put her foot in her own mouth either or dig herself into a hole, or some other idiotic idiom. She wanted to say what she felt and be heard.

For now, she cried.

Chapter Seven

"This is nice," Harper giggled, her heels clicking on the marble entryway as the men showed her to the registry desk. They spoke succinctly in Krussian for her to the attendant and a key was produced. Nikolav grabbed it and turned away from the desk. The inhospitable sounds of the Krussian grated on her from all sides and the mechanism in her brain that loved languages and translating was working hard not to register anything going on around her, save the two men.

"Is he up there?" she asked Nikolav, moving her eyes to and fro on his face in faux-excitement.

"No," he laughed, guiding her by the shoulder to the elevator, "not for at least a day will you see him, and even then..." he let his words trail off and stopped talking.

"Then what?" she asked dejectedly.

Nikolav kept his palm on the small of her back, letting his hand slip lower until it rested on the apex of her curving behind.

He groaned, "Mmmm, very hard to say."

Harper shifted, slumping her body in disapproval as she slipped from under his hand.

Having nowhere to place it, he raised his hand to his chin and said, "He may not come, you know."

Harper got quite close to his face, "Then I should make sure nobody but he touches me, no?"

He handed her the keycard, grimacing, and she returned the look with a smile before she turned and walked away, knowing her hips and legs would move rhythmically whether or not she put effort into it. The elevator came as soon as she pressed the button and she stalked inside of it, hands clasping the gold railings as her purse fell to the ground. She coughed into the back of her hand, choking on the disgust she had felt as Nikolav's hand gripped her. There was nothing sexy about it to her unless she was killing. That was no revelation to her and the knowledge that it was coming made her lips twitch into a smile just as she opened the door to her hotel room, a veritable prison until she met the diplomat and was able to give herself reason enough to check out.

Harper fell on the bed and turned onto her belly, reaching over to the nightstand. She started to smell the melted cheese and old grease. She took out the old cheeseburger, tearing off the yellow wrapper and letting the first bite consume her entire palette. She would have to go back onto birth control, she thought. She thought of Lane and began redesigning the medications she would need to be on to stop either one of them contracting any number of diseases from this.

"That was disgusting," she told herself as a bit of red ketchup fell from the burger. She engulfed the last portion of the food with her mouth and felt the grease linger on her lips.

There was a disquietude in her mind as apprehensive thoughts peeked in and resided there.

Prying the heels from her feet, Harper found serenity in her solace. Her hand delved along her skin to touch her ankle, massaging down. Touching the rough texture of the back of her foot was unconventional for her. Normally, Harper would be mindful of what she touched, aware of the places her hands went and unwilling to sully them on parts of her body, especially when she was readying herself to touch or hold Lane, to whom she never wanted to add any soot, smut, muck, or mire.

Now, away from her love and in the midst of political tribulations, she felt looser, capable of touching the dirty parts of herself. She removed the other shoe, reminding herself that there was a job to do.

She walked over to her carry-on and pulled from it a single box, stainless steel and very foreboding in appearances. Her hands both sat on top of it, then opened it. The equipment was all new, of course, but the agency had taste in these sorts of things.

She was not here to reminisce, but the objects she was holding were of the same merit she was used to carrying. They felt solid and sturdy as she held them in her hands. She didn't have weapons, but she certainly did have equipment. She was mindful of not growing attached to using any of them, nor having sex at all. They were all for sexual play, mostly props to get the clients comfortable. To put them in a false sense of security, Harper would brandish them, touching them to her lips and wiping them across her cheeks. She touched the glass beads, choosing to close the box as hints of longing to have them in her crept to the forefront of her thoughts.

Recalling her original intention, she placed the box in the center of the armoire, closing the doors on it. She sat on the bed, calling for room service to bring her two bottles of vodka, which she would keep next to the box until the rich, white man walked in the door.

"Anything else?" the porter asked.

Harper looked at her foot dangling off the edge of the bed and said, "You know what? I would like a cheeseburger."

"Alright, would you like fries or a salad with that?"

"I'll have both, thank you," Harper told him curtly.

"There will be an additional charge for both," the porter told her.

"Charge it to the room."

Apprehension tore at her innards. She willfully ignored the unease that, by fearing what would happen when it was done, she would not be able to end it. She breathed unsteadily, trying to find peace in something, but was empty-handed. She ran to the bathroom, started the shower, stopped the drain, and laid face down in the tub. The water pelted her behind and pooled about under her.

She breathed in deeply as the water rose and held her face under the water. She looked at the white ceramic as she held her breath, thinking, Is this what dying will feel like? I don't know and won't know until it's upon me. Of all people, I should know.

Hearing the whine of the door's hinges as it opened, she put on a towel and stood watching next to the door as she let a boy cart in the meal. The porter left after having brought the new food up without question.

Harper didn't like letting people leave. She had lived, for many years in a constant state of making sure people always stayed. In her body were the last wishes of countless men, many of which had become tyrants in their countries and many of which deserved to die.

After letting the porter leave, she thought not of the next man she would kill in the sheets, but of the ones from the first year she had begun. After she had come to her commanding officer with the idea to lure prey to her, she had decided to do a few on her own and let the agency she was working for cover them up for her.

Those men's faces came back to her, the faces of men that had realized she was not tormented by their intrusion into her life, but that she had wanted them back again. The burned-in faces spooked her, for she knew she had ended them slowly and without clemency. She had been lenient for years, carrying the stories of their abuse in her where scars did not form. She had carried them with her without reason, until she had realized their potential.

The first man to be killed was not unlike the others. He was a man of power that was beginning a territory war he already planned to end. He was a threat to the entire world and he had been stopped, quickly and without indulgence, by Harper.

Many years before, Harper had been dating a woman, as she always had done. A Mexican artist from California, named Cecilia. Cecilia was more than a decade older than Harper, but she was the woman that had taken all of Harper and had loosened her. She had made Harper a softer person under her touch.

Instead of hearing the sighs and sorrows of humanity as she normally did, Harper heard the laughs and glee of other people when she was with Cecilia. There were flowers blooming on the windowsill of the apartment they kept together, and in the chambers of both of their hearts.

The first time Harper had seen Cecilia, she shook nervously for minutes, sighing, finally, when Cecilia came up to her and asked her if she could sit down. Her black hair fell in curled tendrils past her chest, skimming against her black blazer and drawing Harper's eyes across her body.

The second man had been pimping and whoring out half of Harper's town before finally ending on her. But he hadn't succeeded with her. When he fought her, she resisted and in retaliation, he had taken Cecilia from her, forever, instead.

She had met him again, just two days after she had first killed. Knowing she was capable had made her relentless and persistent in reaching this goal she had locked away deep inside of herself. When she was relentless or persistent, she could do anything. When she was both, she was doing nothing but meeting her own needs.

Harper tossed the balled up trash from the other cheeseburger away, thinking of the new one and rubbing her lips together. She wondered if she killed now for retribution for her past or control over her present. She could end up knowing the answer by gauging the void it left when she was done.

She unslung the towel from around her body as she turned the projector on. The buttons were much shinier and there was no need for a T.V. connection; the projector did it all. She put heavy importance in finding the right movie to watch. She watched the titles flash before her eyes before she made a commitment.

Lights in the room warped and dulled as the movie began. She wasted no time now and pushed the food into her mouth. On the first bite, onions fell from the burger and dangled, held between layers of lettuce and bun. She scooped them up and into her mouth with only her index before angling the burger slightly and meeting it with her mouth. The ketchup and mayonnaise spread out, creating a layer around her gums, cheeks, and under her tongue.

She chewed slowly, moaning above the opening scenes from a dramatic piece about the Bloomsbury group. Likenesses of major literary figures spelt out the most public and disturbing aspects of their lives in front of Harper as she consumed her meal, starting to eat pieces of salad with her fingers before moving on to dip a fry in the ketchup that had leaked from her burger and onto the plate.

Oftentimes too pragmatic to relate to others, she found herself passing odd thoughts around in her head to see which made the most and least sense. She finished the movie with no great satisfaction.

Tonight, she was idly deciding how she would go about convincing other people that the cheeseburger was one of the most well-rounded meals. Every food group was accounted for in the cheeseburger. Her toes were the first to touch the water, and the rest of her followed. There was a protein and a dairy, there was a bread, a vegetable, and if tomatoes were really fruits, one of those too. The hot water wrapped around her. Oils are even supposed to be pertinent, if minimal, parts of the diets, and burgers had those, certainly. She tucked her shins under her thighs and the water splashed from one side of the tub to another. She kept her anti-cogent argument for the cheeseburger running until her mind let it slip from her, like water from a sieve.

She turned her body over and dipped her chest, then head, into the water, careful not to even splash her hair. She held her breath after she had submersed her face and she opened her eyes, staring at the beige bottom of the basin. She lifted herself up and out of the water, gasping for air.

Knowing anything meant complete certainty, and that, Harper had never had. She was a relativist, in denial that truth can be found at all. In her line of work, in a lot of government jobs, you had to have a belief system you were proud of. Being a relativist meant she had never had a problem with receiving orders. Sure, she felt wrong about some of them, but that was only her limited perspective. She was not skeptical about her actions or orders, for there was no absolute truth nor validity to either of them, just a wider frame of reference.

Skepticism about your work came from modesty, and once you had killed a few dozen people, a drop of skepticism in your head was like a tiny pocket of air in your blood; it would go straight to your heart and kill you immediately. No coming back from that.

She lay like this for minutes, hot water scorching her thighs, butt, and back until she couldn't feel the pain anymore. She felt like a masochist, torturing herself for what she had done, and at the thought of becoming something she was not, she got up, turned the faucet, unplugged the drain, and stepped out of the bathtub.

Touching the towel to her face and legs, she tried to grasp for thoughts but they were gone. She had even forgotten that she was trying to forget something in the first place and she idly played with her appearance in the mirror.

Chapter Eight

Fumbling for her phone, Lane faintly recalled already swiping it open and pushing back the alarm. She decried the makers of the phone, the founder of the bakery—of everything—as she skipped her shower and put on pants, a t-shirt, and shoes. She wore heels today, because she missed seeing them on Harper. A passing glance in the glare of the door's glass struck her self-confidence as she realized she also missed the shape of Harper's legs. Lane thought her own were a poor comparison. She took the Oldsmobile, reminding herself to go the dojo that night for a karate class and to not pour water on customers' laps or refuse service to them either during work.

Nine hours later, she was pulling back into the driveway. She rushed inside, heels stamping out little noises that ricocheted off the hard floors. She pulled the shoes off and let them land haphazardly with diminutive thunks. She pulled herself up the stairs and stripped the tight jeans off, replaced her underwear with more practical beige underwear that was less recognizable though the karate uniform. She checked her phone for the time and realized she had time to spare. She switched out her bra for a sports one and padded down the stairs to the kitchen.

She was already moving to the pantry after making a packet of carrots from the fridge. There were four mid-size containers that weighed between fifty to one hundred pounds each when full, which was standard for most homes. If Harper had wanted, she could fit into the jars comfortably. Long gone were the days of individually wrapped foods that people wanted massive quantities of. This month, Lane and Harper had filled the containers with several items, but the dehydrated peas were what Lane sought out first. A smaller bin had thousands of crackers in it and she rummaged in it with a hand until she had a grasp on a large quantity.

She removed herself from the panty and leaned over the kitchen counter, eating what she could as quickly as she could. She put her face under the faucet and gulped the water before setting out to the dojo.

When she got to the studio, she realized that she had purposefully, if not intentionally, wanted to be early. The small seating area in the dojo faced the whitewashed wood floors and mirrors of the place where they practiced. At this time, a children's class was going, conducted by her sensei's wife. She had an easy smile when the children were focused on her, but when she was focused on their form her eyes were stern and rigid as they followed the children's movements. She was the border collie, giving off ease and comfort when the sheep watched her, but when their thoughts were off of her she was in diametrical opposite to the mask of ease.

Lane's sensei worked behind a desk and when she bowed and muttered a formal petition at the ingress, he bowed towards her, unspeaking. She took a seat next to the amused mothers as they watched their children and she thought of them, how they entered the dojo without bowing and saying, "Onigaishimasu." The word rolled over in her head several times before she tried to recall what it meant, not just what it sounded like. It meant a lot of things and, perhaps, was overused in karate to the extent of meaning less than it should, but to her she was saying to them a thanks in advance for being so well taught that they could now teach.

When she thought this, her heart stopped and she looked at her sensei from the corner of her eye. Lane was remembering the way he had touched her. He had guided her arms as she attempted blocks. A blush rose to her cheeks that made her wipe the area with her fist. Pulling out her phone, she found the website for the yoga studio and canceled her monthly membership, without questioning it further than thinking she wanted to spend most of her time here, rather than there.

In class, her sensei again had everyone sitting and was standing rigidly as he explained to them the force that they wanted to have when they kicked as well as the elasticity to remove their foot from harm's way. He opened his mouth then closed it and Lane noticed his eyes fall on her. He stepped far right from where he was standing in the center and swept his hand to the area.

He nodded at her and she reciprocated the gesture. Her hands went in front of her, in a triangle position, and she knelt forward, bowing into her hands, then sprung off of them to step to the front of the room. She bowed to her sensei, then used her best judgement to get into a ready stance for kicking. Her right foot was back, she was in a long stance, and her hands were up. Her body was turned towards the audience of seated guests in folding chairs and karate students on the white wooden floor to her right.

"When you kick from the stance Lane is in, you must pivot your front foot," he said as Lane kicked and she heard the onlookers gasp, "like that. Again, slowly."

She nodded and kicked him slower, finding it more difficult to adjust the angle of her foot in the pivot when she reduced her speed. When her foot was near his head, she heard a gasp from the class. Her sensei lifted his hand and blocked the kick, unperturbed by the mass inhalation.

"You may either block, duck"—he exhibited this—"or grab the foot, which you should be wary of if you are kicking. The more power you are putting into the kick, the more power somebody can use against you if they are quick and strong enough to grab your foot and, say, twist." He did so, knocking Lane off balance and making her hop on the front foot that was still planted on the ground. "Or they can throw you." He made to throw Lane by the foot, but in actuality pushed just enough to let her leg swing safely back to its original position. "Thank you, Lane."

Her feet came together, as did his, into V's at the base of their clasped legs. She bowed to him and he reciprocated immediately, then she found her seat and sat down again, raptly attentive to the rest of his lesson and the ensuing practice of the application.

Driving back home, she felt especially wet and sticky with the excess of sweat and removed the top to her uniform immediately. She felt even more alleviated to be able to walk into the house and begin removing her clothes there in the foyer. She glimpsed her red face in the mirror, shiny still, before she pulled the knot on the pull-strong of her gi pants and pulled them down.

Gasping, she stared at the still-wet blood that had seeped from her vagina, onto her underwear, then through the crotch of her white gi. She gasped, the same revealing gasp that she had heard from the class and audience sitting in those little chairs, watching her kick. She recalled how she could have completely exposed the vermilion pigment. Deeply crimson and spread like a dove, wings unfurled, it was dark and so discernible that she didn't need to let her eyes linger on it to comprehend it in full. She hurriedly balled up the pants, but the stark red stain against the white of the pants was tormenting her still.

In abject and bleak movements, she unadorned the underwear from her body, their own red stain another vivid trauma on her character. She gathered everything and brought it to the washroom, where she dumped a few cups of detergent in with them and set them on a heavy-load cycle. She went to the kitchen, naked from the waist down and only wearing a tank top above.

Passing the note she had left for Harper, she smudged her thumb onto it, leaving a few circular lines of her thumbprint in red. There was so little it dried almost before she had opened the freezer and was opening the lid to a pint of ice cream. She licked the inside of the lid before she got a spoon . Standing there, in so few clothes and with her bright pink face still in shock and embarrassment, large beads of sweat clustering to her scalp, she shook her head and sighed, pushing the ice cream into her mouth as she did so.

Chapter Nine

Harper slept with her muumuu on. Its ruffled sleeves and flowing dress quality reminded her to be a lady. Her apparel was the first thing she thought of as she was awakened only a few hours after she had fallen asleep by a Krussian security detail. Their hands were everywhere, but only for an instant. Ten of them had arrived in her room without warning, and nine of the ten left without warning.

Entering the hotel room, the rich white man Harper had been waiting for was much more important and influential than her sleep-ridden eyes had imagined. She was still lounging in her bed, holding her head straight until she saw him, at which point she cocked it to the side and let her eyes roam up and down his body. She put on the illusion that she was making a choice, and that he had passed. Her ankles clicked together, then her shins spread apart, a sexual mannerism she was making up on the spot, and one she would have to remember if she was going to build up a persona tailored to him.

The prime minister of Krussia looked behind himself to see one man waiting, probably one he knew very well. He jutted his head to have him leave and the man nodded curtly. One he did not want to get to know any better, apparently.

Harper drummed her hands against the bed, eyes stern and fixed on him. He sauntered towards her and took off his shirt at once. Harper knew not to betray emotion and stood, strolling away from him towards the armoire. She laid a hand on it then turned. He was watching her carefully. She knew he wasn't hungry for her. She took a long, powerful step and raised her hand to him, pushing his sternum and watching him fall. He had a strong neck, which is what she usually liked to break. Not only did men love to have their heads cradled, but it was clean and quick. He was still tense, stormy eyes set and tense as he studied her face. Harper's mind reeled as it realized she would have to work harder than ever to get him comfortable enough for her to break him. She thought of Lane's body, soft breasts, and the warmth between her thighs. The imagery got her comfortable with the feeling of having sex.

The prime minister's elbows were against the bed now and he was still looking up at her expectantly. She turned from him, creating an image of her round butt and smooth,

spindly legs beneath it as she swayed them away from him.
She opened the armoire quickly and placed the silver box in
the center of the nightstand. She went back to the armoire
and, turned from him, shut the doors. She unbuttoned the
miu miu's first few buttons and turned to take a long step to
the bed, the silky blue fabric falling to expose her long leg as
she did. His azure eyes followed the shining mahogany line as
she then lifted her leg above the bed and his body, then
pushed down on the comforter and raised her entire body.
She swung her other leg from the ground to one side of the
man's hips. As she approached him, he lifted his pig-skin
hand and gripped her calf, rubbing up into her thigh. She
moved her head back, moaning for him, and she felt him
push aside the fabric near her hip.

Her leg slid up the bed until her ankle was inches from
the cloth of his pants. It was fine cloth, and he hadn't brought
a change of clothes in. But she hoped he wouldn't be leaving,
which gave her every reason in the world to rip it at the
middle seam, which she did. His face betrayed shock as her
hands moved quickly to the area and tore, but her fingers
soothed what was underneath the pants, twirling her fingers
on him like she was twirling a falling tendril of Lane's long
hair. Her hands were off of him after only a moment of
rubbing up and down the stiff area of underwear. She acted
like it was a tease, but she deeply did not want to have sex
with this man. She saw lust in his eyes now; she saw a deep
and overwhelming desire. Her knees pushed into the bed on

either side of him and she lifted up, momentarily away from his wandering hand on her leg. She moved herself so that she could have sat on his chest, tilting her ear to her shoulder and studying his face intently.

She lowered her hands from her hips to her legs, pushing all of her energy and power into her palms and fingers. She was gripping his eyes with her own when she saw the icy blue of his move. She followed his gaze to a tiny red droplet on his chest.

It was a viscous droplet that was dangling from some of his chest hairs and pressing into his skin. Another droplet fell from her vagina onto him. She looked at him, betraying trepidation.

His hands were on her and she felt him gaining leverage to toss her over as he said, in Krussian, "I love it when a whore bleeds."

Chapter Ten

Lane spent her walk to work wondering why it was so stressful to walk past strangers. Lane ducked her head as she passed them on the street. There were heavy moments of indecision as she nearly smiled then averted her gaze. Each new passerby was another chance for her to lift her head and smile, but she never found the strength. Instead, she kept her face down or turned away.

As if hoping to distract herself from the distraction of walking past strangers, she smelled the grass being cut near her, remembering a few lessons from over a decade ago in biology.

One day they had learned that when the grass is mowed the blades release a chemical that makes an intense, almost nostalgic smell, but its real purpose is to warn the other grass blades of danger. As she inhaled, she thought of all of the redolent atoms specifically designed to be screams of danger and warning among a species.

Enthralled, along with her classmates, at new and unimaginable truths, she had listened raptly and with wide eyes, as if yearning to hear with her eyes the certitudes spoken to her class. Often, the veracity of her teacher's statements was called into question in her mind. She got caught up in the falseness or duplicity she, and perhaps only she, perceived.

On one such occasion, her teacher proclaimed that everything humans—men and women—do is to mate. She had cornered that idea many times in her mind, able to see it as both a falsehood fabricated by horny male teachers and a complex but true-to-life claim. It was not an unwavering fact, though, as Harper and she were testament to that. Though same-gender births were a viable option and Harper had already been granted coverage by the government to allow Lane to be the carrier, they had both conceited that it wasn't for them. Both of them had had very different reasons, but they were all valid and their lives were not progressed by the attempt to produce offspring.

Lane looked up, grinning, as she hoped she could talk to that teacher now and let him know how many hours she had spent completely at a loss and disconcerted thanks to his teaching. She caught the eyes of a stranger and forced a larger grin to spread as she nodded to them.

When she got to the bakery, she noticed it was slow again and sighed. She enjoyed the ambling around languorously, but she found she acted more childish when there were less people to be serving. She threw herself into bagging cookies, then wrapping brownies in stamped butcher paper before letting herself loosen up.

"How's your essay going?" she asked her coworker.

"What?" he asked. He looked up and away, then back at her. "Good, good. I'm on to studying other stuff, though. I've been thinking about how people just talk about moonshine like it means nothing."

Her hands paused and she opened her mouth to say, "Uh-huh. They do."

"Well, there was definitely a time when you couldn't even get close to that kind of topic. To talk about that meant you would have the feds searching your house and watching where you go. But now, if you talk about it, I don't know, it's socially acceptable in a way that I bet people during prohibition never thought it would be."

"It makes you think about the things we're currently experiencing and how different they could be."

"Exactly my point," he said, carrying the tray of plastic-wrapped cookies away to the collection room. When he returned, he helped Lane's brownie project. She told him what she had learned about grass-releasing chemicals when it was cut. He thought it an invention of her mind and checked it out on his phone before shrugging and putting it back in his pocket.

"Seems you're right," he said, "which is just so wrong because we actually enjoy that smell. But it's just tons of little plant screams. Imagine if another species was killing us and we were screaming for mercy and they just thought what beautiful music it was as they painted portraits of each other with our blood."

Lane laughed. "That's sick!"

"It could be a future we live in," he said, walking to the counter to take a customer order, then retiring back quickly. "When was the last time you were in school?"

"Ten years ago," she said, laughing. "It is something I was actually just thinking about."

He looked at her, incredulous, and said, "Really?"

"Yeah, why?" she asked.

"Well I took an exam and I noticed something tickling my throat, so I coughed a few times. Then a few seconds later, I had to cough again, but I didn't want to keep disturbing the people around me, so I sat there, spending precious minutes of the exam basically suffocating and choking myself to keep from drawing attention. It was this weird, torturous, awful experience that I would not wish on anyone. You are lucky to not be in school, with that kind of pressure there."

"Rubbing your ears can relieve an itchy throat," Lane offered.

"Really," he said. "That is some useful information. You should be a doctor."

"Don't say that, I had my chance to study something and my window of opportunity is gone. No doctor job for me."

Her coworker looked away thoughtfully then filled the silence by saying, "Humans have evolved into a niche of thought no other animal has attained. Funny that we all play on the same evolutionary field, but only one species has found a benefit in thinking as much as humans have.

"There must be some reason to it that even our thinking brains have not ascertained. What if there were a hundred animals besides ourselves that thought on our level and reasoned with our scope and whose brains have progressed on a path paralleling ours? We would not be so arrogant, I'm sure," he finished.

Lane looked to him throughout, then looked down at her work wordlessly. She thought listening to yourself speak to prove something exists when you admonish it is more admonishable than the thing itself.

He shrugged and sought the twine to tie the brownies up. When he left, her fingers slipped and covered a brownie improperly, but Lane shifted it away from the rest and told herself she would take it home.

Sirens blared outside. Her coworker came running in, bug-eyed. He gasped and spoke as he ran from her, "Air-strike," before continuing to run.

"Is it a drill?" she asked as the air horn blared. He turned back to her mid-stride and shrugged. Harper began running towards the back as he did, afraid she might see him trip and need to pick him up and carry him to the back cloister. All of the businesses surrounding the back cloister, including the bakery, had deposited all of their workers and customers to this area and they sat, shoulder to shoulder, speaking in soft whispers and yells. Steam rose from their hot, almost over-exerted bodies as they regained composure after their quick and mortal run.

Lane's looked for familiar faces in the group, but resigned herself to putting her knees close to her chest and letting her eyes fall away from the onslaught of reality. She did not rest there, but remained unmoving and tensely immobile. She did not want to watch the drones move in or away, today. Her fingers felt like Harper's would, putting pressure on her shins and thighs as she held the whole world away with her own stout thoughts.

Deep vibrations quivered from the base of her spine and butt and moved up her, slowly following her bones and nervous system as she registered the trembling. Her eyes were hot and she felt tears germinating and sprouting from her eyes, falling in fruitful bundles. She looked up, registering the shock and concern on everyone else's usually composed faces.

"Lane Trill!" came a rushed and tight voice through the crowd.

She stood quickly. "Yes! Here, yes!" She saw a man, the only one standing, in full military uniform. She felt worried for him, standing and moving about in this situation, but as he beckoned to her with a hand to stand up and walk with him, she realized that she was about to become someone others felt concern for.

He validated her consternation by saying, "You're to come with me."

"Yes, sir."

"Do you have your things?" he asked when she was close to him.

"No," she added apprehensively, "sir."

His stern face grew impotent as he let some of his power over the situation grow. "Would you like to get them?"

Her body threw strength into her legs as she ran into the bakery's ingress, clutching metal and scaffolding as she did. The soldier followed her and was close to the entrance, taking a bite out of a cookie, when she ran back out the exit.

"Let's go out the front," he said nonchalantly and Lane's shoulders dropped, feeling impuissant.

She followed quickly along behind him, around the trembling and clattering baking equipment. She looked behind and above her, worried about falling items.

"We really have much more secure residential areas," he sighed as he opened the glass door for her. Her eyes swept the area between road and sidewalk for an obvious government car, but she was rigid and transfixed. She had to be ushered to the big black jeep by the man.

She got in and buckled the racing seat style belt across her chest, taking her phone out of her purse and sitting on it before dropping the bag at her feet. The soldier got in the car quickly and drove away from the area with resolution written on his face.

She asked, "You know my name, what's yours?"

"Name or title, Mrs. Trill?" he responded with a clipped tone and a question of his own.

"Name."

He said with a clenched jaw, "Mrs. Trill has us under strict orders to keep our identities out of the ears of civilians."

"Mrs. Trill being my wife?" she laughed scornfully.

"Yes, Mrs. Trill," he glanced quickly at her as he spoke.

She shook her head. "That's dumb." He glanced at her again and as they drove she made some noises of excitement and pointed to their right. "Please take this street, please, please."

"For what reason, Mrs. Trill?"

She said, "I need to make sure something's still standing."

He followed her orders and turned the car. She looked at her dojo and the surrounding street, standing fully erect. She pressed her hands to the plexiglass of the window as she looked in to see if her sensei, students, or his wife were inside. She saw nothing and the lights were completely dim. She sighed, a mixture of relief and trepidation. She could see five angular drones spread out across the horizon.

"Are those ours or theirs?"

"See how the shape is triangular and not a quadrangle? That means they're ours," he informed her.

"Then what are they doing? I felt an explosion."

"Suicide bomber in the underground."

She calculated and spoke, "That's not Krussian, then."

"No, but we are in a word war, ma'am."

She clenched her jaw. "It seems we are."

After they had parked, she got out and collected her bag. She looked away from the car, to her home. She was happy to have had an excuse to get away from work, she thought, bitterly reprimanding herself after doing so.

"Don't forget this," he said. She looked back as he handed her phone to her.

"Thank you," she said as she held it in her hands and walked to the door. When she was inside, she began to turn on the projector and sat down with the tablet, saying into it, "messages".

A list of mail appeared on the screen and she began removing some and reading others before getting to one that made her pause. She set the tablet down on the couch and leaned over it as she slowly said to herself, "How did I overlook this? How could I have?"

She dropped her hand onto the tablet and rolled it up in her hand, clutching it to her chest as worry and water etched places into her eyes.

Chapter Eleven

Harper's hands found the place below his skull on his neck. Her face exuded comfort as she pushed with one hand and pulled with the other. The Krussian prime minister's reaction was delayed. His eyes bulged in some semblance of understanding only as she dropped his head, lifting one leg and gliding it through the air until it clasped the other.

She slapped his face, "Calling me a whore. Meet your maker, mister." She pushed off of the bed and glided over to her bag. She grabbed the wet napkins and wiped down the surfaces of the room, then pulled a 4 oz. container of bleach out of her bag and emptied an ounce of its contents onto his chest, where her period had decided to begin. She pulled the blood off of his skin and out of the curling hairs on his chest with the wet cloth.

"That was disgusting," she said to herself. She put the box of sex toys she hadn't used into her bag, probably a better prop for her than for him, and changed into a pair of pants and a sleeveless collared shirt. She gripped her old-school tennis shoes and struggled to get them on. She much preferred heels but not for this work.

She thought for a quick moment that she could get out the door, knock out the ten or so guards and walk out the hotel's entrance, but she chuckled at her own exalted view of herself. "Never did learn krav maga," she said to herself, berating her lack of motivation to learn the world's deadliest fighting tactic which all of those men knew better than she could fathom. She pushed herself up onto the desk and stood, unscrewing the fasteners with her fingernails. She collected them in her hand and rummaged in her bag for a tiny stick.

She crawled into the air shaft, one foot first then the other as she held herself up with her arms. She brought the cover with her and pressed the stick's back-end button as she held the air shaft's cover in place. It spot welded each corner and she crawled backwards until she reached a T-intersection in the shafts and diverged, able to crawl forwards. She moved quickly, feeling a deniable sense that the prime minister's guards had found him. Nothing except instinct gave her this feeling.

A smile flickered on her mouth as she became overheated, thinking that it was funny because she was about to be very, very cold. When she got to an air vent that tunneled down, she held the sides and slowly de-escalated. After going an appropriate height down, she knocked out the first vent that showed natural light from the outside. She looked down, seeing a revving box-truck directly under her.

"Excellent," she said as she jumped to it. She had been right, it was cold outside and the metal of the truck was no exception.

The driver of the truck pulled over and she jumped onto the cab of the truck and broke the passenger's side window with the corner of the hard metal box she had in her bag. She pushed the sensitive point between the driver's collarbone and shoulder with her thumb and watched his head slump. She moved his body to the passenger's side seat and checked for a pulse, smiling when she felt it.

A mile out of the capital, she brought the stainless steel box from her bag, wiped it down, and threw it onto the highway where it jumped under the chassis of one vehicle and tore the wheels of another.

She drove herself to the U.S. Embassy and found herself on a flight to D.C. to debrief.

"How did you like it?" asked her commanding officer.

Harper's jaw was set as she said, "I didn't have sex with him, sir."

He asked her, "Oh, come on. Really?"

"I'm good at my job, sir, but if I can limit the danger I put myself in, sir, I will," Harper said.

"Do you not enjoy the job anymore, Trill?"

"I enjoy executing the desires of the U.S. government, sir," Harper said sternly.

"But you don't want to have to do the"—he stumbled for words—"dirtier aspects of the job anymore?"

"No, sir." She felt something inside her fall apart when she said it and her shoulders slumped noticeably.

He chuckled. "You've changed, Trill."

"For the better, I hope, sir."

"You're not as useful to us on that island."

She said, "I would like to be of best use to the United States, sir, and believe I am doing so with my position on Cuba, sir."

"Having a facade of power is not useful, Trill, and you know it." He looked at her closely as he spoke.

"The highest position in the United States government is then as useful as mine, sir." Her tongue was certainly in her cheek now.

He let her get away with the statement and said, "I want to talk about reassignment, but before I do I want to know what makes you happy being there."

Harper's jaw readjusted and her shoulders tightened. "The line of danger has lost its appeal, sir."

"I like to respect when someone under my command goes into the business of having a family, Trill, but that doesn't seem to be what you're doing."

"I do not want to add to a world that I haven't helped perfect, sir."

"Ideologies have no concern stepping into my office, Trill." He turned and walked towards a glorified painting of battle, saying, "either you start a family or you go back to working the field."

Fighting back emotions, Harper looked for alternatives. "Is there a different line of work that would better suit me, sir?"

He turned and walked closely to her, containing his speech until he was inches from her. "Harper, goddamn, you just exterminated the man strangling the free world. You better understand how much of an asset that makes you. No, we won't retire you to stand in front of a classroom. We're going to pimp you out to every goddamn man that wants to take you. Understood?"

"Yes, sir."

Chapter Twelve

Calling the dojo, Lane was relieved to hear the sedative voice of her sensei answer, "This is Goju Ryu, Sensei Jal, speaking."

"Hi," she began, "This is is Lane Trill, I'm a student of yours." She heard the muffled grunt of his response. "And I was wondering if you're still open today."

"Yes, come in."

"Thank you," she said.

"Arigoto gozaimasu," he said, correcting her or thanking her, she did not know.

"Arigoto gozaimasu," she said in reply and disconnected the call. Hurriedly, she changed into her karate pants and tank top, folding the uniform top and belt into her gear bag. She smiled slightly as she changed her pad in the bathroom and rushed out of the house, revving up the car and making her way there.

She bowed in. "Onigaishimashu."

He bowed to her, stacking papers and bending over forms at the desk. The dojo was empty and she began warming herself up. Hands on her hips, she spread her feet outwards then inwards ten times. She stood on the balls of her feet, then shifted her weight to her ankles, swaying her hips. She saw his eyes on her from the mirror's reflection and stretched her legs, bending one completely and letting the other straighten away from her body. She leaned against the bent knee and went low, skimming the floor with her belt as she did. She pushed against her thighs and switched to bend the straightened leg and lean against it, straightening the alternate leg and listening as her belt hit the floor, again. When she was done stretching her legs, he strode to the front of the room and motioned towards the floor. She knelt, feet placed under her butt as she closed her eyes.

"Mokuso," he said and closed his eyes. They sat silently, in quiet meditation. Sometimes, in full classes, he talked to the students about reflecting on the class they were about to have and what skills and training they were preparing for. "Rei," he said and they bowed to one another, hands in triangles on the white washed wood of the floor, foreheads dipping low to nearly touch the back of their hands. "Sensei ni rei," he said and she bowed to him, slowly lifting herself up to look at him.

"Not too many people in class today," he said, beginning the class more informally than normal.

"No," she replied tersely.

"Do you think anybody is afraid today?"

She hesitated, remembering the faces of those in the cloister behind the bake shop, then said, "Yes."

"Fear's presence creates a void."

"It does?" she asked.

"A void is not natural," he said. "A void needs to be filled. You, today, have chosen to fill it with something. What is that?"

"Practice," she said, studying the recesses of her mind, "which is bunkai."

"Only perfect practice makes perfect," he told her. "True, yes?"

She nodded, "Hai, sensei."

"Bunkai is practice, but more so the application of karate techniques. You do that everyday. Or nearly everyday." He smiled to himself. "I did it everyday for a long time without knowing the reason I did it; the reason was there, but I didn't learn its name until a very long time later. It is bukido."

Lane repeated the word, "Bukido." Then, to tell him she didn't understand, she said, "wakarimasen."

"It is the warrior's way," he said. "I understand you have a wife in the military?"

Her face became stoic as she said, "Hai."

He inquired, "She knows the way of bukido?"

Lane did not know it, but Harper was on a plane and, at that very moment, was deliberating on her food item. Harper ended up asking for both meat options and struck up an informal, quiet conversation with the woman next to her. Lane imagined much worse things for her wife as she strongly said, "Hai, sensei. She does."

"Now, do you?" he asked her.

"No, sensei."

"Do you want to?" he asked.

"Hai, sensei."

"Good!" He slapped his palms to his legs and stood, "kiotske!"

She stood quickly, eyes fixed on themselves in the mirror as he showed her a lower block. "We will do this, but with contact."

She nodded and they began on his count. Their forearms locked and twisted away from one another with heavy loads. His arms were like wooden planks hitting her, and after twenty she noticed a serious dwindling in the physical force she exerted. He paused, slapping his inner arms, then rolled up his white sleeves. She mirrored him, rolling up her sleeves, then slapping the red, tender flesh.

He counted again, from ni-ichi, twenty-one. They went until go-ju, and, because she had loosened her mind's grip on her actions and was simply moving as well as she could, Lane did not know that was fifty. He switched feet and said, "Ashi kaete." She nodded demurely and did it. "Too slow!" he said. "Pushups. Go!"

She did not ask how many, but pushed her feet back and gripped the ground with the area between her palms and fingers, pushing up and down until she had counted to ju— ten—in her mind. She stood back up, quickly putting herself into a ready position. "Hajime," he said softly and they began hitting forearm to forearm. There was an iota of added ease now that they had switched the arms they were hitting and she relaxed into the movement, focusing more on the words he was saying and less on registering the pain she was receiving.

"Now," he said, pulling a blue tumbling mat off the top of the stack of others like it, "you know the roll we do? I want you to practice that on and off the mat."

Lane wiped a rolling trail of sweat that perched on her eyebrow and streamed down into her eye, stinging it marginally. She nodded and watched him demonstrate the roll on the mat, slapping the ground hard as he fell, rolling his shoulder so that only one side of his back struck the ground, and whipping his legs over and under to stand. He did it wickedly fast on the mat, but slowed his pace and talked through it as he did it on the softwood of the dojo, reminding her the importance of tucking her chin to her chest.

"Try it both ways—let's say, five times."

She approached the blue mat and bent a knee, hit the hand on the same side of her body as the bent knee, and tucked her head in. When she bent her shoulder and made contact, pushing through it, her legs followed. She stumbled and stood.

"Shake your legs out," he told her. She did, then did the same series of movements on the wood. The back of her feet slammed into the wood and she registered shocking pain near her spine. "That was too slow," he said. She looked at him, aghast, and he explained, "if you move faster, there will be less contact with the ground. I'm not saying that because I have high standards, I'm saying it because I want you to excel." She nodded, rolling quickly on the mat, then, with a stutter in her step, turned and did the same on the wood. Her heels landed properly this time and she stood quickly, relieved. "Again," he had to say to her and she turned to the mat, ducked a shoulder, and sprung from her heels downward, spiraling, then back onto her feet. Her muscles had memorized the routine already and she was turning, kneeling, and rolling on her shoulder before she had asked herself to. Her body stung, the origin unknown to her, as she rolled and the nerves somehow became poor transmitters.

"You barely contacted the ground with your shoulder that time, but did with your hand. Very good," her sensei said as she did it on the mat once more. She rolled in almost the exact same way as she had on the wood previously, and he had her stand at attention after she had.

"I was bicycling up in the mountains one day with my son," he told her. "I had turned a corner and there was a rock in my path, directly below my front tire. You may think I am perfect, but mistakes come in life to everybody. My bike had stopped before I had time to steer away from it and I was flying through the air, in front of my handlebars. I knew I would hit the ground, and so I was ready when I did and hit it with this exact roll I am teaching you now. There were plants and trees and rocks there, but when I fell, I knew what to expect from doing it so long that it did not surprise me. I surprised my son by standing on my feet just as quickly as he had seen me fall, but I was not surprised. That is how good I want you to become. Practice this at home?" Lane nodded her head once, vigorously. "Practice this at home?" he asked again.

"Hai, Sensei!" she vociferated.

"Good. Now put this mat away and we will do one more technique."

She bundled the mat up and lifted it above her head. "Hai."

"Stand in front of me, hands on hips, and, with your right leg, hit the inner shin to mine. Same as before. Very good." He talked her through it, which was an extreme solace, because the duress her body was under was making her tremble and shake. Her brain was no longer being sent the majority of oxygenated blood and she could only think about the ligaments, bones, and muscles under harassment.

"This is not too much," her sensei said, a bewildering statement that should have been a question. Lane shook her head, no. She kept thinking of his statement, a motto filling her head. She kept thinking it until it dissolved into a decision that nothing was too much for her.

She swung her leg wider and hit it hard against his, an onslaught of pressure he seemed to neither enjoy nor be at any detriment from. She looked to him, stoic and long-suffering, and lowered her gaze from his eyes to a point in his chest, focusing on the area where the two white sides of his gi met. They continued this until Lane lifted her hand to wipe sweat off of her forehead again, and her sensei's eyes flickered from their practice to the clock.

"Let's finish up," he said and they both returned to the center of the room. "Mokuso," he said and they closed their eyes. Lane found her breathe return to her as she ever so steadily regained composure and before she was able to reflect on the class, her sensei had said, "Rei." She dropped her head and pushed her hands forward, looking up from her bow as she sat straight to see her sensei smiling at her kindly. "You did some very difficult and strenuous activity today, but you didn't give up and that is very important. Remember what I said about bukido, and find out what perfect practice means to you. Do you have any questions?"

Lane nodded, enthusiastically speaking cold words that chilled her. "Sensei, what if bukido, the warrior's path, is not for me?"

"Then you would not be here," he said knowingly, "but that is for you to decide, not to find out when it is too late. Thank you, Lane. Arigoto gozaimasu."

She was saying the formal Japanese thanks as he began and she bowed to him again.

Chapter Thirteen

"They can't delay my flight by twelve hours," Harper said to herself. "This has to be a conspiracy." She knew it was not, though, because she had been warned that this could happen. She looked at the window with an air of hostility, but she knew better than to become quarrelsome with the weather. She felt pugnacious and quarrelsome, though. With an ambition to find resolve, she paced away and back to her original position near the glittering wall of flight schedules.

She pushed her heels into the cold marble and into one of the spacious airport breezeways. The reverberating clicking of her heels made their course from floor to her ears as she checked the time mindlessly. She propped herself on a chair, still stamping her heel, but now it got her nowhere.

"Monotony," she said to herself, knowing it to be one of the killers of her own thought processes. Idly, she turned her wrist over, noticing the shiny vertical scars on her wrist. She watched them sparkle in the light before throwing her wrist down to her side, telling herself inaudibly not to romanticize the harm she had inflicted upon herself but to move past it.

She pulled her bag to her side, still feeling the need for the adrenaline and endorphin rush she had once been able to give herself at a moment's notice. Seeing a bar, she approached and waited. The bartender was busy, but when he saw her he presumed a lot and walked towards her.

She inhaled, gulping for air, then said, "One piece of ice, please."

"I can't just give you a—" he started to say, but she found a twenty in her purse quickly and pushed it to him. He continued, "Coming right up." The tinkling sound of the ice did not soothe her. She wanted to hold it.

He put three on the wood bar in a tumbler and she took just one out, gripping it firmly. Immediately, the feeling of distress and fear were pushed from her and she smiled, relaxed. A nurse had given her the tip to do that a long time ago, when she was recovering from cutting and anorexia, and she was overwhelmingly grateful to have had someone there to tell her a technique, not just to stop.

Let the cold fill you. Let the pain open you up, if only to see that it has no place in the warmth of your self.

Fog banks rolled in. Ocean storms were brought to the swamp town. Flights were delayed. She threw herself towards the window, watching the clouds furl and unfurl. They were gray as a newspaper, with black dots and places of obvious tumult and dissent like that of the black typefaces. She saw in the swirling masses nothing picturesque, nothing beautiful. She saw it not, but it was all there. She watched, though, regardless of whether she consciously enjoyed the sight.

Falling prey to watching the movement and animalistic nature of the planes, transport cars, wagons, and ant-like men and women on the airstrip, she walked even closer to the window, breathing softly until her breathe hazed the window and blurred it with its moist, dewy fog. She only noticed the droplets were accumulating when her vision became unclear. She stepped back, perturbed, to see she had created the tiny cloud on the window pane. She watched it, obsessed with seeing the dimples and malformation in her vision she had caused.

As humans, we are obsessed. We love to know what it is that charms us, what it is that can take us over, and what it is that we can destroy.

Clearing the window of its newly acquired dampness, she saw the lights in the distance twinkle. Idly, she remembered Lane had asked her why that was as they looked out across New York. It was a few years ago when they had gone and, enjoying only some aspects of the city, they had never gone back. But that night, in the hotel room's twentieth floor, they had looked out of the window together.

She had said to Harper, "Why do the lights twinkle?" in a child-like voice.

Harper had answered quickly as she walked towards the window, "Stars glow a certain way when they're coming towards us and a different way when they're going away, like how a fire engine wails loudly when it's approaching and not so much when it's going away. Light and sound have a higher tone when moving towards, then the frequency lowers when moving away from you and the wavelengths get longer." Harper breathed heavily after she had explained it away.

Lane, ever patient, had waited until Harper was done to change her own way of phrasing. "Not just stars. I mean the city lights twinkle and sparkle, even when they're not moving. But, only when they're somewhat far away. Not when they're this close." Harper approached Lane and looked where she was looking, to the stray residential towers, streetlights, office buildings, and bridge lights.

"Lane, I don't know."

Lane looked up to her. "Well, will you look it up for me?" She watched Harper momentarily before traveling back to watch the luminous movement along the city.

"Of course." Harper had her tablet in her hands at full tilt and spoke the question into its microphone.

"I like that building over there," Lane said amusedly, but Harper was not looking.

Harper said into the tablet, "Speakers, please."

It spoke in a calm, placid voice, "The light refracts as it passes through air of different density."

Harper said, "Isn't that interesting?"

"So the further away it is, the less you see of it?" Lane asked.

"Well, yes." Harper thought quickly, then said, "I guess that doesn't apply to stars, because they're in a vacuum."

Lane asked with a soft whisper, "Space?"

"M-hmm," Harper muttered.

"I thought space wasn't a perfect vacuum because of dust?" Lane asked.

"How," Harper began to ask, then changed her mind to state instead, "you don't know that," and changed her mind again to make a question of it, "do you?"

Lane muttered, slowly, "You said it once."

Harper said, "I guess I forgot about that."

Lane said, "Did you know that only light can travel freely in a vacuum? What is it, water and sound? They can't do that. Travel freely. They can't."

"No, I didn't remember," Harper said.

"I heard it," Lane yawned, "certain—" She had not finished yawning.

Harper said, "You sound tired. Want to go to bed?"

"Not to sleep," Lane said to her as she picked herself up from her position next to the grand window.

The memory flooded Harper as she stood, staring out at the twinkling lights of the airport and, further, of the city. She wanted, more than anything, to curl up in a warm bed and sleep off some of the heartbreak and pain she was hiding from herself. The scoundrels she let out when she was working, when she was with rich white men, when she was killing— those scoundrels needed to be put to rest for a time.

Searching for something far away and without a place she knew of, Harper stalked from the window, from the terminal, towards one to the other, until finally she found a storefront with an appealing premise.

She walked in, past the empty and large recliners with their small baths beneath them. She walked past an empty reception desk, shifting her hand from her purse to a stack of towels. She grabbed two and held them under her arm.

"Hello?" she called. "Anybody in here?"

There was not a stirring in the entire place. She had walked into a spa, with signage promising massages, pedicures, manicures, and showers. She scanned the area worriedly, looking behind herself to see the normal stream of civilians walking quickly about the airport.

"Somebody, anybody?"

Her feet were moving her further into the spa premises without her consent, but she did not stop herself. Pushing no doors open, she only went where doors were ajar. Finally, she chanced upon a large shower room. Only one shower occupied the entire space, a room the size of a kitchen.

Harper gave one last cursory glance, then walked in and closed the door. She smiled as she locked it, then stripped and placed her purse and the towels on a hook in the wall far from the shower head. Delicately, she removed her heels and placed them on a stool, wiggling her toes as they touched the small tiles of the ground.

The knob of the shower turned squeakily and she shuffled away from it. She bent at the waist slightly to extend her arm to feel the water. The droplets hit her hand and she removed it, shaking them. The water was hot quickly, but the water pressure was so high she was worried her nipples would be shorn from her body by it. She released the knob and it became like a person weeping on her. She stood underneath it, feeling the soft trickle of warm water down her back. She sighed and turned it on the higher blast, feeling the hot water lash out at her and wrap around her muscles and ligaments, search out her bones, and push past her veins. She felt encapsulated then and there, fully wrapped up in the sensations overcoming her.

Chapter Fourteen

Lane sat over the dining room table, re-reading the message. It told her about the commemoration for her ex-girlfriend, Ashna, in California. She had loved her, perhaps she had broken her heart, too.

Her finger played idly over the screen as she thought about all that it meant to her. She looked at the time stamp and realized it was happening in only a few short weeks. She knew she would not attend. The lingering anticipation for it was there, though.

She awaited the day that it was held, daunted by her own emotions. They had both been but fifteen-year old girls when they had loved one another. The heart shape comes from the cut Silphium plant, an ancient Roman contraceptive. Mild arguments are good for healthy and developing relationships.

Dryer Detergents are made out of beef fat. The autonomic nervous system senses emotional cues and after pain or stress, activates the nervous system, causing nausea and visceral pain. The US government has mirrored Roman structures of government with separation of powers, a constitution, checks and balances; even, before the collapse, the wealth holders refused to pay higher taxes. If by some stroke of genius you were to know all of those things, you might also know why it is so much fun to fall in love while you're young.

Especially so when, to impeccably brilliant people, you have fallen.

Stricken, Ashna had removed herself from Lane's immediate life quickly. She had gone on the pretense of going away to a college, but there was no knowing. Not with the way she had died.

The tablet slid across the table as Lane pushed it and she found herself drawing pictures of men throwing snowballs on paper. When she had finished, she wrote on the bottom:

I remember you telling me about the biggest snowball fight in history that was between the Texan and Arkansas members of the Confederate troops that escalated to include something like ten thousand men. I remember things like this, instead of thinking of how I love you so.

xoxo

She put down the pen and pushed the paper towards the center of the table, sitting with her hands under her chin. Her eyes went out of focus and she, feeling quite indolent, didn't focus them back. She stared at nothing, taking in the sights around her as shapeless, formless colors. When her eyes happened to move, she could see most clearly of all small specks and spots. Her face was placid, reflecting not the turmoil and disease in her mind.

She worried for Harper, for her safety and her mindset. In her reasoning, her worry was important and necessary. She feared that if there was no fear, terrible things would fill the void. But, if she thought of all the terrible things that had possibilities, she could realistically erase the ability for it to happen. So, she validated her concerns and thought of those as she stared at absolute nothingness, thinking of so many more things than what could happen.

Breaking her from her reverie, a child's voice pierced her ears, saying, "What is nine times six?"

She went to the window and replied, "Thirty-six."

The voice from next-door traveled back to her, "Thank you, God!"

"Not God, but you're welcome," she said out the window and turned away.

"Lady, then, fine," came the squeaky voice. "What is nine times seven?"

Lane sighed, then yelled, "Add nine to thirty-six."

The squeaky voice asked, "What's that?"

Lane bellowed from the window, "Figure it out, kid!"

"Not so helpful, Lady," came the reply, carried on the soft breeze of the day.

"You're welcome," she said to herself as she walked away. The sudden disturbance from the outside world gave her the idea to put on sandals and walk outside. Outside, the air softly brushed her shoulders and pulled her out of the shallow reverie she had begun embarking on when she was inside, surrounded only by the objects that reminded her most of Harper.

Harper, unlike her, sought to be alone. But when Lane was alone, she was not in such control of it. It was not one of her demands of life, to be left alone. She wanted, more than anything, to run next door and hug the child that had called out of his window. She wanted, as she thought of that, to go to the dojo and hug her sensei. She, in hopes that she would slow her thinking by outracing it, got into the Oldsmobile.

She took the turns and straightaways without hurry, lapping up with her eyes the sites. There stood homes unlike hers in architecture, but very similar in that they held in them people and lovers. Some of them held families, unlike hers. She touched her finger to the volume dial and within moments found herself shouting along with the music.

Her throat grew hot as more and more sounds escaped it. Squinting to bellow during the highest notes, she found herself holding back a stream of tears. She kicked her foot as she waited at a stop, stomping to the beat and holding her mouth closed, now. She pushed back the emotions the song brought about in her. She pushed them back to sit in her belly, then lower into her tailbone. She shook her hair happily, resuming the song as the light turned green for her.

Cuban city streets were packed, filled with lines of cars that gradually, then all at once, began moving. The cars were a mixture of old and very new. The cars that picked Harper up were quite often the newest town car or luxury SUV, an odd testament to have an acronym that includes sport and utility when really, a tiny fraction of the vehicles were actually used for such purpose. There was an odd mixture of cars on the streets. New sports cars clung close to the ground while older cars like Harper and Lane's seemed to push away from it, still barreling through the street at the same pace since they were stuck in the same lines and at the same lights.

Until the animals stopped having sex, it seemed Cuba would always have an aggregate of animals exceeding any other American State. Donkeys, mules, and horses looked either an untidy disarray to the side of the street, or an attestation to their worth in a modernizing society. The industrial age's collapse would either fall on their shoulders or break their backs, though. The former was the optimistic desire of the people there. Lane clicked her tongue to a horse standing next to the car and its ears flicked towards its back. The blinders it had on and the rigorous set of chains and bars kept it from turning to see her, but she had expected to comfort the animal as they both waited.

At the green light, the whip tapped the horse's back and it began trotting and at once galloping with a speed from a place Lane could not identify with. She longed to be running, pushing away from the world behind her. Knowingly, she stayed in her car and made a choice more attainable.

She pulled into a space in front of the school, its front walls jutting from the sidewalk for four stories before the curling and twisting facade finished. It was painted white, but the years had seen many colors on the colonial front.

Walking up the steps, she became disoriented at the desk, where nobody sat.

"Hello?" she called into the inner cloister, where a fountain babbled.

"Oh? Well, hi!" came a disembodied voice.

"I'm here to see about admissions," she said.

A woman in a bell skirt and pearl necklace that pushed up at her jutting collarbones and contrasted brightly with her skin came in from the cloister. She extended her hand to Lane, shook her hand, then smiled and sat down behind the desk. "Admissions? Our classes don't start until this date, here." She pushed a calendar into Lane's hands. " Although you can take our admission tests today." Lane breathed in sharply. "Oh, don't worry, they're just placement tests. Are you thinking of taking any math or english classes?"

"Not this semester," Lane told her.

"Then we can forego them." She handed another piece of paper to Lane. "Fill this guy out here and we'll process your request for admission immediately."

"Thank you," Lane told her.

"Have a seat over there, if you will," she said to Lane.

Lane sat down, scanning the paper and began filling out the general details. She was confused about one question and tapped the piece of paper, as if she were trying to zoom in on her tablet.

"What did I just do?" she whispered to herself. She set her elbows on the table and held her head in her hands, laughing a little at what she had just done.

"Lane? I didn't expect to see you here," came a voice. She pulled her hands down and looked up to see her old coworker.

"Hey, hi. How are you?" she asked.

He put forward the question, "What are you doing?"

"Oh, just being weird." She withdrew her attention from them, then restated, "well, signing up for classes."

"Really? You should take one with me," he offered.

"Your classes seem to be a bit above what I'm looking at," she said with a steady gaze on him.

He asked, "What are you going to take?"

"Hopefully some general education classes," she told him.

"Really?" he said, "that's great!"

"How's your day going?" she asked him.

"You know how this school still uses paper for most of the coursework and"—he pointed to the paper Lane was using—"admissions, apparently?"

"Yeah," she agreed, the validation to his point being forthright.

"Well, this girl in my class finally, finally, finally asked me for a piece of paper today and I had this marriage certificate printed out like, the second day of class. So I handed that piece of paper to her."

Lane's nose crinkled as she laughed and said, "You must have been so embarrassed!"

"No, Lane, I mean"—his hands flopped around in front of him—"I was, but I had planned to do that, you know?"

Lane guffawed, jaw and hands falling towards the desk she sat at as she decided whether to laugh with him or at him., "I can't believe you!"

"I really did it. She sort of looked at it and smiled, then asked if I had another. I told her that was the only piece of paper that mattered to me."

Lane told him, "You totally lost all of your chances."

"I feel bad for girls—women—because you lose a lot of time in your lives talking to men that you're really not into and being scared of their reaction if you deny them," he said.

Lane grew serious as she said, "So what, you do something so weird they have no way to respond?"

He groped for words. "It's almost like I know I'm going to get shot down, so why don't I shoot myself in the foot and that way I can blame myself, not them, for not liking me?"

"Girls are constantly accommodating men and boys as a means of survival, because men don't take rejection peacefully in all instances," Lane said, "so if you can hit on a girl with your tongue in your cheek, letting them know you completely accept failure as an inevitability, or at least an option, it helps take the societal pressure off of us."

"I think that, too." He held the back of his neck with a hand, looking to a distant place. "Or, at least, I try to. I've had my patience and gentleness stripped away from me by this big bad wolf that is society. I thought Cuba was different."

"No, no it is not." Lane laughed bitterly.

He sighed, then pushed up his glasses. "Well, I'll let you get back to your admission forms. If you ever want to grab a coffee or something, I'm around here a lot."

"I'll keep that in mind," Lane said as she turned back to her forms.

When she was finished she turned them in to the woman at the desk and drove to the cliff, parking to watch the sun dip into the sea. Stars came out and she tried to remember how Harper had told her something about stars. Whatever it was, it was to do with their ephemeral blinking, she knew that much still.

She found she had just enough time to make it to the last karate class of the night so she went.

Chapter Fifteen

The words pierced Harper's ears out of a deep reverie in the shower. "Paging Mrs. Trill to the front desk located near terminal O. Paging Mrs. Trill to the front desk located near terminal O."

"Those"—she turned off the shower and ran to towel off and throw her clothes back on—"buffoons!"

She was clicking through the hallways again, then was asked to board a private line to Cuba, ready on the runway.

"Sons of"—she found herself saying, but as she was hit by a strong breeze outside she recollected herself —"daughters."

"Would you like anything from the cart?" she was asked once stewardesses were allowed to pass throughout the jet.

"Yeah, alcohol."

The stewardess looked at her, laughing into her palm. "This is a dry flight, ma'am."

"You have to be——" Harper put her headphones back in and looked away from the woman to the drop-down screening of a television show, then finished muttering, "just kidding me!"

When she was on the ground, one of her staff was waiting for her. He asked her, "To the office, Mrs. Trill?" She would not be going there, where her permanence was in question and where she had already wasted years of her career playing the paperwork game.

Harper replied coarsely, "I'll be going to my home, immediately."

"I drove your wife back home during yesterday's bombing, Mrs. Trill," he informed her.

Harper noticed her staffer calling her by her name now, whether it was because she had actually gone into the field or because he had met Lane, she didn't know. "I hope you didn't rub off your PTSD on her."

"Madame, please," he said, seeming mentally wounded by her.

She searched her mind for a way to reconcile, but realized there was absolutely no need. "Your trauma is caustic, sometimes."

He sighed out words, "I didn't share anything, ma'am."

"Good. Well, thank you for taking her and me back," she told him, then with a change of tone, added, "feel free to take the rest of the day off."

He replied humbly, "Thank you, and good work out there."

Harper's jaw set sternly as he said the words and she tilted her head, shifting her body to get out and walk the stone path to her home. She opened the door to see a bit more disarray than she was used to, but smiled as she was picking up to find a number of notes from Lane on the dining table. She shuffled each one into a pile and took them to a wooden box in her office, where she kept all of the notes like these from Lane. Her hands worked quickly to move the pile and find one of her favorites. She read it then closed the box, leaving the letter on the top . Her hand moved from the note to her chest as she left the room and continued to pick up, following a trail of cast-away clothing until she was close enough to the bathroom to hear Lane inside of it. A jar rattled against the counter as she knocked and opened the door.

Lane's jaw fell and her eyes did the smiling, creasing against her cheeks, before she said, "You're home, you're home, you're home!"

Harper spread her arms and Lane bounced into them. "Did you just get back from class?" she asked Lane.

"Yep," she smiled smugly, her bottom lip receding into her mouth.

"Which one?" Harper asked.

"Karate," Lane said, "the Goju Ryu."

"What's that mean again?" Harper asked as she rubbed her shoulder, arms, then hands.

"Hard and soft style."

"Very impressive, Lane," she said as she stopped massaging herself.

Lane smiled. "Thank you, or, arigoto gozaimasu."

"Arigoto." Harper mimicked.

"No, no. That's too informal," Lane told her. "Gozaimasu means you're a professional."

"Well," Harper shrugged, "are we professional?"

"Only if you're my prostitute!" Lane giggled. Harper's smile became forced and she let it fall completely as Lane turned away from her to shake out her hair in the towel.

Lane turned back to her, asking quickly, "You in the mood for some she-bang, she-bang?"

Harper turned and shook her head once, not saying anything.

Lane smiled. "That's why I asked. I know it's hard to adjust right when you get back. I haven't been for a walk in ages. Want to maybe—"

Harper was licking her lips, catching on. "Can we please go to the garden? Can we, please?"

Lane smiled, tilting her head back. "Oh, yes we can. Clothes or no clothes this time?"

"Oh, shut it! I'll give you a minute to get dressed. I need to make sure there's nothing damaged around the house, anyways."

"Oh, you shut it! I took good care of the place while you were gone."

Harper laughed as she exited the room. "Like hell you did."

She walked into their bedroom, basking in the soft purple light from the curtained windows. It smelled of so many scents that she could no longer place just one; they were a collective. She purposefully walked to the nightstand, opening its only drawer, and looked down to see her strap-on. When she saw the black chords and purple latex Harper breathed in deeply and exhaled with a smile. She closed the drawer and walked to the hallway, picking up random objects and placing them in their appropriate places.

Lane giggled on their walk, saying, "So what can you tell me?"

"Well..." Harper inhaled sharply. "They want me in the field more or making a family."

Lane inhaled. "They gave you an ultimatum?"

Harper smiled grimly. "That they did."

"Is there some kind of time limit they gave you for the field work?"

Harper shook her head, watching their feet as they walked, and gripped her hand around Lane's elbow.

"The field work," Lane asked, "is it the same sort of stuff?"

"Yeah, same old, same old."

"Well, is it still dangerous?" Lane asked.

Harper's voice grew an edge to it. "Yes, Lane, it's still dangerous work."

"Not"—Lane looked around the desolate area—"black ops stuff?"

Harper snorted. "No, those people are freaks."

"More like freaky," Lane said, raising her eyebrows suggestively.

"Don't bring that up," Harper inserted quickly, then laughed. "I still can't believe what they did with those shrunken heads."

Lane nudged her with her shoulder. "Come on, you had fun."

"I plead the fifth," Harper said. "So I saw that you cancelled your yoga thing. What happened there?"

"Oh." Lane sighed. "Not much, they just have this no-touching unless you specify you want them to."

"Tell me more," Harper said.

They were at the gardens and gathered trowels and spades. Lane shrugged as they walked on. "They don't have anything going on like that at the dojo. They mean business there."

"So they," Harper said, "touch you at the dojo?"

Lane looked away, saying, "Only the sensei."

"How?" Harper wanted to know and used a hungry, terse tone with her one word.

"To help with my form and techniques. I'm actually really sore after today's class. I think I'm developing a series of bruises up and down my body from it all."

"What did you do today?" Harper asked, quickly clipping Lane's words.

Lane shrugged. "Conditioning. We did some one-on-one combat stuff. He had us do katas, which I didn't like as much as hitting another person."

Harper's blood felt like it was running cold for a number of reasons. "Laney," she began.

"I know you're worried about me getting hurt and all," Lane said.

"It's not just that," Harper said.

"Then what?"

"I'm worried you might like it."

"Being touched by a man? Harp, it's not like that."

"Not like that, no. The combat aspect of it. The—" Harper lost her words.

Lane found some. "I'm not going to want to work the way you do. Or do it anywhere outside of the dojo. Sensei teaches us not to use what we learn outside of the dojo, not even if somebody attacks you. You can still talk to them."

"Lane, when I started to learn combat I used it all the time, even when it wasn't appropriate."

"Well, you may have been less mature than you should have been when you learned." Harper put no refrain on her words and was not concerned with how Harper took them, as she felt Harper was prophesizing that Lane would do poorly.

"That aside, it presents a new spectrum of concerns for me to feel, and I'm having trouble choosing whether I should or should not be concerned," she said.

Lane touched her chin with her hand. They were both standing outside of their plot, and Lane bent over to kiss Harper quickly on the lips. "It's something I'm discussing with you because I don't want to hide it. I thought you would be upset that I'm letting a man touch me the way he touches me—"

"Just—"

"—not sexually, right. But now that I know your concerns are elsewhere but still related, I will think hard and long about those."

"Good, Lane. Good."

Lane puckered her lips, saying, "Bad, Harper, bad," then kissing her more deeply. Harper loosened her tight muscles and let her tongue meet Lane's.

They pushed and pulled the soil for a good portion of the hour until they had cleared an area. They went to the seed bank and selected a few starts from the vending machine, then took the small plants and put them into the ground where they had been toiling.

"Want to do the honors?" Harper asked as she handed Lane the watering bucket.

"Would I ever," Lane said as she watered around each tiny green sprout. "You know, I've been thinking."

"About what, pet?"

"If the general guy—"

"Not his title," she said, "but go on."

"If he said you need to start a family or work in the field..."

"You can't be saying."

"Are you open to it?"

"I'll go to the clinic tomorrow and get my genes arranged for it, Lane. Yes, yes, I'm open to it!"

"Oh, I thought you would want to sleep on it and say no." Lane bawled, hands in her face.

Harper moved forward and encircled her arms around her. "I don't know what I would do if I had to be kept away from you for another instant. At least this way we can give them good reason to keep me here."

Lane looked at her with vast yearning in her eyes. "And?"

"And I want to see another human get to experience this love and joy that we have." Harper looked back into those exhaustive eyes of Lane's, hoping for a plan that would work.

Chapter Sixteen

"At this time you could not have children, Mrs. Trill."

Harper's eyes grew ardent, moving quickly as she sparked out words. "Why is that?"

The clinician looked over her records. "You seem to have contracted a sexually transmitted disease."

"That makes sense. Have you looked at my file?"

"You do not seem to have a file, Mrs. Trill."

"That's odd." She thought, I used to have one. "At any rate, my partner has always been on medication to prevent her from contracting my disease and I am aware of the circumstances."

"You do know—"

"I know everything about myself. You do not, and so I would refrain from telling me about myself unless you want to find a difference in your paycheck this month. Verify that I may have children with my wife or excuse yourself."

The clinician adjusted a pair of red-rimmed glasses and smiled nervously. "Your eggs have been spliced into a pseudo-sperm and on file for the last five years, Mrs. Trill. If you would like to take some home today, there would be no hindrances."

Harper asked, "They can't be fresh, why not?"

"No, unless you want the specialists to be brought in from mainland. We would have to wait at most a month for your cycle to get back to the ovulation, but they could be brought down. Whether or not they can be transferred to sperm, at this stage of the disease, is another question only they can answer."

Harper put a face of confusion on. "This operation is no longer public, is it?"

"I'm afraid, due to war-time efforts, a lot of things are not public services that may once have been."

Harper pushed her tongue against her cheeks, wondering when the cessation of the war would come now that the Krussians were crippled. It was important to her to know that citizens were allocated appropriate resources like this one.

She said definitively, "I'll take the sperm."

"Would you like an M.M., Harper?"

"You don't have a right to call me my name just because you're touching my vagina once a year. Let's keep this on a professional basis, please." Harper added, quickly, "What's an M.M.?"

"Mitochondria mutation, ma'am."

"That's no better. What is that, the designer baby thing?"

"Prevents against mutations. Most schools only take children with them in the genes."

"No, I will not."

"You can't always change your mind later," the clinician said before Lane pursed her lips and wagged her fingers as she held her head up. The clinician left momentarily and returned with a white box the size and look of a lunchpail. She opened it to reveal dry ice surrounding the container of sperm.

She said, "Dry ice is for foreplay, right?"

"What? No, no. It is to preserve the—"

"Hey, I'm relieved I got it and was making a joke. You can suck a dick, right?" The clinician looked baffled. "Well then, you can take a joke."

She put the box on the kitchen counter with a note that read, "Do not touch," and went to work.

At the offices, reports were stacked on her desk, waiting to be repurposed or filed. Her office plant needed watering. There was a layer of dust on the windowsill that had settled in her absence. She wiped it off and said, "If dust is skin particles, where did these come from?" She looked to the ceiling and said, "is old skin clinging up there and falling down constantly?" She almost said, "that's disgusting," to herself, but the memory of saying it before was enough to halt her. She sat down and became occupied in the reports.

Chapter Seventeen

"Lane," said her manager over the desk, "I need you to explain to me what happened during the routine disaster the last time you were here."

"I was called out by—"

"Exactly," her manager cut her off. "You left work early. Now, it's out of my hands, but that's a strike against you."

"Alright," she said, "I am sorry, but you see—"

"No excuses, Lane. One more minor infraction, the smallest thing, and you're fired."

"Great. Thank you."

"For what?" her manager said.

"Taking the time out of your busy schedule to apprehend me," Lane said with a shrug, standing up and leaving the room. When she got into the break area, a group of coworkers were gathered around the table.

"Lane! We need your help," said one, ecstatically grabbing her shoulders.

Another: "Yeah, we've been waiting for you all morning."

"What is it?" she asked.

"We need you to draw!" said a small girl she worked with.

Another one said to her, "Yeah, It's Justine's birthday and we need you to make her a card."

Lane put up her hands. "You know what guys? Birthdays aren't really my thing."

"What?" they all seemed to ask, bewildered at her.

"You need to, though," said the small girl.

Lane smiled, cornered. "No, I try not to celebrate them. They're just...against the way I try to celebrate."

"No, no," they all seemed to say. "You need to. Just draw it. For Justine."

Lane shook her head, sitting down. "Fine, fine. Get me a piece of paper and a pen."

She sat for five or ten minutes and drew a picture of Justine, her sparkling smile, her long ponytail falling past her hips, and her hand on her side. She put two banners over and under her, reading, "Happy Birthday!" on the top and "You don't need to be told you're amazing, but here we are telling you: You're amazing!"

She handed it off and wasn't there to give it to Justine.

"What do you think about religious holidays during winter?" asked one coworker of Lane.

She laughed. "Presents are nice and all, but I like to remember the real reason for the season, being Persephone's descent into the underworld." Her coworker looked aghast and Lane laughed, saying, "I was joking!"

At that moment, another baker approached her, saying, "Lane! You need to give Justine something."

"What do I need to give her?" Lane asked.

"Whipped cream! A whole plate of it!"

"Really?"

"Yes, yes! You need to," she said to her.

Lane said, "Why don't you?"

"I already gave her something! Here." She handed her the whipped cream container. "Go!"

"Okay, fine. Whatever. You sure she wants this?"

"Yes!"

Lane then ran to the back where Justine was sorting cookies. "Here you go!" Justine gave a yelp and ran past her into the front. Lane, dejected, ran into the front of the store. Justine smiled and hid behind a refrigerator. Lane rolled her eyes. "You know you want it."

Lane pushed the cream onto Justine's nose, then threw the plate away and walked back to where she had been working, concerned that her coworker had gone crazy and that Justine had to undergo that, whatever it was.

"Lane," her manager called to her hours later, "My office."

Lane trudged into it. "You wanted to see me?"

"Please, sit down," her manager said, holding a tablet under her face.

Lane did and said, "What do you need?"

"Just a minute," her manager said, holding up a finger. Her manager finished reading the tablet and rolled it up, disposing of it in the trash.

Her manager spoke steadily, pushing the words towards Lane's concerned ears. "We need to talk about the whipped cream incident."

"What about it?" Lane asked, feeling less strong than ever.

"You went too far," she said.

Lane felt herself held together by a thread. "I don't know that I did."

"This isn't open for discussion. You went too far. You have consistently shown an irresponsibility and this is what it has come to. Whether it's because you're not focused enough or are just this way, I don't know, but it doesn't work in this bakery. The owner has asked me why I keep you here when you act out in these ways and I can't keep saying that I don't know why. We need you to leave. Here is your last check." She slid it to Lane.

Lane held it in her hands, idly thinking, then tore it in half and let it fall. She watched it fall, thinking, Arguing can be both horrific and cathartic. Hearing things about yourself that someone else has seen and thinks for true should be an indulgence of great measure. She blinked back tears, both gracious and perturbed. Reminding herself of the sadness of the matter, she thought, horrifying, though, to hear them said in a vain desire to wound you.

"Lane!" her manager yelled at her as she stood up.

Lane left through the back egress, happening to see the owner of the bakery. "Are you leaving or coming?" he asked her.

"Just leaving," she said coolly.

"Oh, okay. Good-bye." He had small, round spectacles and was generally a nice person. Her visions of burning the bakery to the ground or having Harper buy it from under them and leave her manager out of work left her as she saw his smiling, cabbage patch kid face one last time.

When Harper got home, she saw Lane on the couch eating ice cream out of the pint and asked, "What happened? Something happened."

She put her head in her hands. "I made a terrible mistake."

"You quit your job?" Harper asked her nonchalantly, setting her things down and assessing the state of the room. Pillows sat on the couch, disheveled, along with Lane.

Without thinking, simply happy Harper was so close, Lane began to quickly reply, "Mhmm. No, I got fired. For giving someone whipped cream, I got fired!"

Harper stepped over couch cushions to sit next to her. "Lane, pet, you have to admit that sounds really funny."

Lane pouted. "It's serious. I act so childish sometimes."

Harper sighed and wrapped her arms around Lane's shoulders. "Lane, you didn't have that job other than to take up some of your spare time, remember?"

Lane sniffed as she looked away. "I still messed it up."

Harper pushed away from Lane's body to show her a very serious look on her face. "No, they messed you up. They were working you too hard and, personally, I want to work on robots taking over those type of dumb, mind-numbing customer service jobs, anyway."

"Is that what you do in D.C.?" Lane asked, a smile twitching against the bottom corner of her cheek.

"Yes, pet, I make robots and I can't tell you about it." Harper smiled behind her raised index finger, saying, "shhhh, it's a secret."

Lane laughed, giggling, until she began crying.

Harper asked softly, "Are you on your period, too?"

"Yes," Lane wailed, then asked seriously, "is that why you didn't want to have sex?"

Harper's eyebrow twitched, but she smiled and moved her head to the side as she said, "Yes."

Lane moved her legs to lay above Harper's and asked, "Can we have sex anyways?"

"If it'll make you feel better," Harper shrugged, "yes."

Lane smiled and said, "I want to finish the ice cream, first."

The whites of Harper's eyes noticeably shifted as she looked at the ice cream. "Want some help with that?" she asked.

Lane dug her spoon into it and put it in Harper's waiting mouth, saying, "Sure, it's brown sugar banana flavor."

"They sure don't make ice cream the way they used to," Harper sighed lightly before taking her first bite.

"I like this way better," Lane said, pointing to it with her spoon.

"Mmmm, it tastes like spiced rum," Harper said.

"You think so?"

Harper put her hands on Lane's face. Seeing the dark brown of her skin contrast with the light pink skin of Lane's cheek made her think of the Wilbert Gough quote, "In marriage, being the right person is as important as finding the right person." She smiled sadly, knowing that the void that every human filled with bad intentions and detrimental behaviors was over-filled in her line of work. She was proud of the way she kept up a genuinely supportive and enthusiastic relationship with Lane, at the cost of a work environment that tore her up from the inside out. That pride allowed her to look at who Lane was, and she passively thought of her wife's imperfections and limitations.

"You know this happens every time," Harper said, ushering Lane into what she hoped was closure.

"What, something in this movie?" Lane asked, spoon poised under her mouth.

Harper laughed. " No. Every time I go away you lose your job."

"Seriously," Lane said, "do I really?"

"Your happiness is attached to me being around," Harper said, jaw jutting forward in pride.

"No way," Lane laughed, "I am such a weakling!"

"At least you don't cry yourself to sleep in front of the T.V.," Harper cooed, jaw dropping in faux-revelation as she pretended to study Lane's face. "What? You do!" She jumped to stand over her, taking the spoon and ice cream out of her hands. "We need to start therapy, at once!"

Lane giggled and raised her hands to hold Harper's as she pushed her body towards her. Harper pulled her up, lifting her completely off the couch, and gently leveled her feet with the floor.

"May I have this dance?" Harper said as she raised one of Lane's hands with her own and let her elbow crook into her waist."

Lane allowed herself to be moved around the living room in a relaxed dance along with the music number being projected around them. "You're sickeningly saccharine, my love," she told Harper as her head dipped and fell on her shoulder.

"Your jests are music to my ears," Lane told her, slowly swaying her hips with Lane's and letting the flashing images projected on them force her eyes to close as they swayed.

"Don't you—" Lane began as she felt Harper grip tightly around her waist.

"Dipping!" Harper smiled, forcing Lane's knees to buckle gently. Lane's dark hair fell from around her face and her eyes shrank into tiny slivers as she went backwards. Harper pulled her back up, sliding her hand down as she did. Lane gave a slight shriek as Harper held her under her butt, but sighed resignedly as she realized Harper was lifting her completely now. She looked down to Harper's raven face. They held one another's gazes and Harper's smile pushed her cheeks above the bones that held them tightly across her face. Her eyelashes dipped and, in a flurry, blinked and then stayed wide open.

They kissed, meeting lips and not separating for many moments. Both of Lane's hands held Harper's face and neck under them and her knees squeezed tightly around her hips. Harper couldn't help but smile, their faces pressed and moving against one another, making her smile quite unseen as she wished she could lift her hands up and grasp Lane's face in them as well. Her fingers twitched and she realized where they were, accepting that she had a wonderful grip there instead.

"To the bedroom!" Lane yelled as she lightly tapped her heels against Harper's sides. Harper laughed, grinning as she put both arms around Lane's hips and, gripping her butt with both hands, ran across the living room, through the dining room, and up the stairs into their bedroom.

Chapter Eighteen

Lane stirred the pink salt in with her yellow cherry tomatoes and cottage cheese. It looked worse than it tasted, and she smiled delightedly after gulping down a mouthful. Before she lost herself in eating breakfast, she made sure to ask Harper, "Are you going out of state again?"

Harper shrugged over her tablet, stopping her perusal of emails to answer, "May or may not. I might go further than that, but I don't really know until it happens. I'm hoping and praying that they got my hint and aren't going to send me out, again, but they rarely do give me the gift of at least letting me know what the next year of my life will look like, let alone my weekend, you know?"

Lane looked out the window, her eyes menacing, and Harper rolled up the tablet and tucked it away to focus on her partner, concernedly listening as Lane said, "You should know. They should definitely give you more warning."

Harper laughed, thankful it was something so simple. "There really is no warning for these sort of things. They ask me to do this stuff as it comes up. Hopefully nothing will come up for a long while, again. Maybe they'll give me leave…" Harper stopped herself from saying any more and went back to reading, idly asking, "How are you going to fill your days now that…" Her words trailed off.

Lane twirled her fork in front of her, watching it shine. "The college is always a good place to take classes," she said.

"Yeah, so?"

"I might take some classes," Lane said, smiling at her now. "Some child development classes."

"What?" Harper asked, putting down her utensil.

Lane began straightening the bun on her head and said, "I think it would be a good idea to know the things that are important."

"The things that are important to know if you're going to be raising a baby," Harper verified.

"Yeah," Lane nodded, chewing and eating simultaneously. "Is that a good idea?"

"A superb one, Lane." Harper used soft words and reached over to hold Lane's hand quickly, then squeezed it and said, "so, having second thoughts?"

Lane looked up, creasing her eyebrows together to form vertical lines between them. She moved the food in the front of her mouth with her tongue and swallowed before she harshly said, "No! Just the opposite."

Harper did not smile, saying, "I know, I was joking."

"Oh, I don't quite get it," Lane said.

"I knew you wouldn't. I don't know why I said it." Harper's eyes shifted to the styrofoam box on the counter. She immediately realized what she needed to say next and didn't stop herself. She had to actually make a conscious effort to stand up, walk to it, and point at it, then say, "this is my cum."

Lane's eyebrows raised excitedly. "What? You did it already!"

Harper's face was stony, a fully erected facade against the truth as she said, "I can get more if this first round doesn't work out. Take these pills a few hours beforehand to make your egg drop."

"How exciting." Lane's eyebrows lowered quickly. "Why didn't we use it last night?"

Harper looked away from her wife, unable to read the dejection written on her face, and she began consciously lying to her. "Honestly? It grosses me out just a little bit too much. Even if it is mine, it's been altered to be like semen. That's just ew."

"You know what they say the best part of being a girl is?" Lane quizzed, standing.

"What is?"

"Kissing other girls." Lane smiled and tucked a kiss under Harper's lips. "Now, get out of here before I take a turkey baster to the mouth."

"No, Laney," Harper said in faux-concern, "you know you don't put it there, right?"

"Harper, I love you, and I'll be thinking of how much I love you when I rub one out, okay?"

"You're vulgar, you are," Harper said as she left the house.

Lane sighed, propping her head on the table with her fist as she looked at the little white box. It was so austere and bare, holding a resemblance to something clinical she would see in an office.

She reached her hand to the orange bottle and unscrewed the white lid, dropping the oval pills into her hand before throwing back her head as she swallowed them dryly. She pressed her palms to the dining table, smiling, and stood. She grabbed her gear bag and put a clean uniform in it, nearly skipping on her way to the dojo.

Chapter Nineteen

Near the window to Harper's office came the bleat of a cow, its mooing low and short. From a distance, a sound of a return call came from another cow and the one near Harper's window shouted back to it with a stunted moo. Harper leaned her hip to the sill, looking outside at the trotting beast as it found parcels of grass and nibbled at them.

"Trill, you know I can see that you're not paying attention."

Harper glanced at her phone, smiling at the image of the commander. "Yes, sir."

He rubbed his palms together and his smile wavered as he spoke. "There is a mission here in the states I want you to attend to before your..." Harper's commander faltered with words, then regained composure, finishing with, "leave of absence."

Harper held her phone close to her face. "Sir, by all intents and purposes I plan on discontinuing my work for an indefinite amount of time."

"I know that, I do, Trill, but you have proven yourself time and time again. You're the only operative in the field doing this kind of work and your qualities are, so far, unmatched."

"Sir, if I may point out that I had remonstrated my ability to teach others years ago. If I had the opportunity to do so we would not be having this conversation."

He nodded frugally, tipping only his chin. "When you came to me as a cadet, full of passion, ideas, and adamance, trust you me I thought you were going to revolutionize our agency." Harper hadn't regarded this work as revolutionary. She had seen problems that needed alternative solutions, but now her self-regard swelled. "No need to get choked up, Trill, you have done a worthy job, but the higher-ups don't like the idea of what you're doing being that well known. For the protection of the justice system, we need you to be the first and last of your kind."

Harper watched the cow amble away to join a horse as it nipped its legs, fighting flies as they pricked its skin and ate its scabs or drank its blood.

She had never quite liked being told she was special. That only helped her and the person telling her. She required the world being special. She reasoned she had lost the opportunity to do that.

"I need not for you to extol of my abilities, sir, I just need a job that I can carry out without disrupting my family, sir."

"I'm trying to tell you, Harper, there isn't one for you anymore." Harper looked away from the Cuban morning scene playing out in the warm cloister to look into her phone.

"Sir?"

"You are relieved of duties."

"Thank you, sir. Thank you," Harper enthused. "Does this mean…?"

Her commander smiled now, looking into the camera on his phone hopefully. "This is goodbye, Trill. I wish it could be in person, but these things are for the best. I'm very happy to see you moving on with your life. It has been a pleasure having you serve our nation."

"As it has been a pleasure serving under you, sir."

He nodded and Harper watched his hand come towards the screen as he swiped it and the video call was disconnected. She let herself breathe in the air outside of her office as she set herself on the windowsill and sat peacefully.

Leaving a place gives you a revitalized appreciation for what it is. Confusing as it was, now that she no longer had to look out this window, she began to like the landscape more with every passing moment. Knowing her entire outlook had been brightened, she thought about her limited prospects becoming something much more grand. The smell of hotel rooms and the feeling of men's bodies would be something she would not have to be presented to deal with continually.

Looking around her office, she planned to pack nothing, and took only her phone from the desk and slipped it into her purse. Her eyes caught on one aspect of the one painting in the room. The red orb in the center of it, painted with acrylics and of little purpose to her now, made her hesitate and remember the dripping of blood onto the Krussian prime minister's torso. The orb had both glimmered and been shaded, oozing slowly, consistent with the viscous nature of snot.

"So, disgusting," she said as her back arched downward and the weight of her purse carried her right arm towards the ground. She felt her control of her body slowing trickle away. Her hand faltered and she tried to spring it to action but it hit against the corner of the desk. She held it there as her other hand held her eyes and forehead. Fluid moved through her face and compressed her skull against her skin as her nasal cavities filled.

She cried for her own misdeeds. The way her commander had said others would find her actions amoral tore at her incessantly. The future she had with Lane would always be shadowed by what she had never told her. Worse yet, what if she told Lane, finally conceded to the simple pleasure of honesty, and Lane rejected her?

The future may or may not have held Lane saying, "That's disgusting," in just the way Harper told herself, but she cried as she imagined it, making a cogent argument to herself that there was no other way for Lane to react to the truth of Harper's corruption. She cried after all lucid and vacuous reasons alike had fled her, for the pain of crying hurt her head and made her face feel sabotaged and far from her body as her hand twisted to cover her eyes. She hid herself from the world. A pain and torture nobody but she knew about wracked her body and she slipped her feet from under her, pushing the chair near the desk aside as she fell to the ground, cowering over her spindly legs as she pressed both palms deeper into her eye sockets.

Chapter Twenty

"Harder," Lane's sensei told her.

"I don't think I should," she said. Since inseminating, Harper was consistently worried and nervous that something would go wrong for her.

He shook his head, sweat dripping from his face. "Ten more."

She punched again, counting aloud each time her fist made contact with the wooden plank. It was not the kind of training wood that broke, but one wrapped in leather that stayed solidified and unbroken after the past year of knowing it.

Lane's center of gravity was much different and her feet slipped under her as she let out the last punch. She watched her hand grab for the plank of wood as her eyes widened. She saw her sensei's face remain unchanged until her elbow was in line with his hip. Only then did his hand snap from behind his back and grab her at the crook of her arm. Her entire mass was held up by his hand.

"Thank you, sensei," she said.

"Forgetting where you are is not going to help you in this life. When you are driving—" He stopped, then asked, "do you drive?"

She nodded. "Yes, I do."

"When you drive, you do not think that you are in the car behind you or the car to the side of you, or the car ahead of you. Because if you do, you start to react as if you are those cars, not in your car. But when you picture yourself as being in only one place, the place that you are, you do not react improperly. Do not think of yourself as already hitting the wooden plank before your fist has reached it."

"Hai, sensei."

He turned to the class, ushering for her to sit back down. A few other students gave reassuring glances and nods.

"Now, purple belts and higher, stay standing. I would like for you to learn the kata you must know for your black belt tests."

There were two collective sighs in the room, a sigh from the group of students that led themselves to the side of the room and watched, and an exalted inhalation from those that were to learn a new kata.

Lane stood, readying her feet into the V position and placing her hands flat against her thighs.

"Rei-bow," said their sensei. Every student's hands slid from their sides into pointed positions above their groins, left hands on top of the right.

His voice was strong and guttural as he said, "Kata gekisai dai ju."

The students repeated him, their voices becoming robust in union.

"Ichi," he said and the black belts went into the first position. Harper watched them and moved into it fluidly. Her back leg was bent fully. All of her front foot's weight rested on the ball of the foot as her heel pushed up, like a woman in bed will position herself. Her elbows pressed into her belly as best she could and her hands were bent at the wrists, as if pressed against the same pane of glass.

"Ni," came the sensei's command and half of the group slid into the same position, just facing an alternate direction. Walking around the room, the sensei moved hands and repositioned legs with a low voice. When he came to Lane, he sniffed inward and tilted his head. She pressed her feet lower and he tightened each wrist towards the other individually, forcing her elbows into her sides even more. She looked to him for mercy, but he pushed on her hands, making sure they were solid, and walked away.

"Not having a strong stance means not having a strong kata." He looked to the group of lower-belts on the floor. "What is a kata, Murray?"

Murray, a teen boy with a yellow belt answered, "Isn't it a bunch of different blocks and stuff but in a pattern, sort of like a karate dance?"

The sensei's eyebrows shot up and he smiled at the black belts. "I would say he's right, would you?" They smiled and nodded, then, realizing they were still in a difficult position, cringed and looked down at their burning legs or to the mirror. Lane held her own eyes in the mirror, lowering her butt and feeling the burn of the muscles as they asked for forgiveness. She gave no mercy.

At the closing of class, her sensei reminded them of an upcoming trip into the mountains of the Southeast. "I want you to go," he told Lane personally.

She thought of what she had been learning in child development classes and, though the curriculum was not specifically geared towards warning against travel in early pregnancy, the urging for safety was prevalent and stigmas remained.

The sensei's wife had been in the class as one of the students and, dabbing her forehead, approached them both and smiled, saying, "You really should, it's quite an experience. Being in the hills is the best place to get your mind and your body centered and strong."

"Is it?" Lane asked, regretting not being able to talk to Harper about it until that evening. She said, "Let me think on it, maybe ask one of my professors what they think."

"Whatever you need to do," her sensei said.

"Maybe my wife can come? If it's more than one day I would really prefer it if she did."

Her sensei's wife looked to him, pushing her mouth far up on her face. Her sensei did not look to his wife, though, and remained focused on Lane. "That's not a bad idea," he said. She bowed to him, then to his wife. As his wife bowed, her blonde ponytail bobbed in front of her sunken head and Lane registered it quickly, then turned on the balls of her feet and strode to the black Oldsmobile. She changed quickly and drove to the college, where she was taking a nutrition course.

"Now," said the instructor halfway through the lecture, "what is a good source of calcium?"

A few students raised their hands, including Lane.

The instructor called on a girl in the front row. "Cow's milk," she said.

Lane sighed, raised her hand higher, and listened to the instructor praise the answer. Lane waved her hand. "Sesame seeds, almonds, and white beans are also great sources, as well as—"

Her instructor moved her hand in the air. "Oh! That's enough, enough. Incorrect."

"What are you talking about? I researched this and besides, to be absorbed calcium needs a small amount of Vitamin C, which milk does not have."

"Well there, you're just wrong," said her professor.

Lane looked at the woman incredulously. "You can't be serious," she said.

"Oh but I am. My question now is why are you so serious?"

Lane said, "Because this isn't just a question on a test, it is a rule that you're making that these men and women are going to go home and live their lives by. But you're not even right. Look it up on your phone, there are many different sources of calcium. Besides, saying what is a good or the best is an extremely subjective way of looking at life's questions."

"Oh my," said the instructor, "I wish there were some way to calm you down but, seeing as there isn't, I'm just going to move on."

After class, a friend she had made through another class came up to her.

"Hey, this lady can get a little power trippy," she said. "I'm sorry you had to butt heads with her."

"It's fine, it is," Lane said. "I just enjoy behavioral psychology and actually learning the phases of development so much more than this biased stuff. The other teachers make it so much more fulfilling than this class."

"I hear you there, but remember when we were learning that different weeks of pregnancy correlate to different growths in the baby? One week it could be growing its legs and you raised your hand and asked if it would be a good idea to go for runs and exercise more during that particular week?"

Lane said, "I remember."

"Well, the point is, I do, too. Having people like you speak up more in class helps people like me a whole lot."

"Really? That does make me feel better," Lane said. "After I get in arguments I get all shaky. I just know that's not good for me or the baby."

"No, no it's not. I have to get going tonight. Do you have any more classes?"

"None," Lane said.

"See you in a few days," she said. Lane waved and looked around the classroom before leaving. The professor caught her eye and raised a finger at her, but Lane looked away and walked out of the classroom.

Chapter Twenty-One

The first thing Harper asked Lane when she was home was, "Have you taken a pregnancy test this week?"

"I've been checking all day on my phone," Lane said.

Harper nodded, smiling. "And?"

"Inconclusive results." Lane shrugged, dropping her gear bag.

"Will you try it on the tablet?"

Lane nodded, looking over to it, then said slowly, "It'll probably work that way, sure."

"Will you take a bath with me?"

"I was just going to mention that we take a shower, because I'm still sweaty."

"No bath, then?" Harper asked quickly.

Lane laughed out. "Not unless you want to bathe in some briny human soup."

Harper leaned over the counter, kissing Lane's cheek as she did. "Just test it before you come up," she said.

"I will. One more thing, Harp," Lane said.

Harper looked at her. "What is it?"

"Are you free for a trip this weekend to the mountains?"

"I—" Harper's words caught in her throat and her mind grew convoluted with all of the things she wanted to tell her about her job, as she had wanted to for weeks, but the words held themselves down and she only said, "yes, I would be able to go."

"Great! Oh, this is good. I'm going to have to miss some child development classes, but you wouldn't believe some of the things they're teaching. I'm glad to take a break from this teacher."

"I thought you liked your classes, " Harper said.

"Some of them. In this class I've got an antiquated crone teaching me."

Harper shrugged. "Then quit the classes," she said.

"Harper," Lane began, "It's nutrition and she teaches psychology of play, which neither of us know the first thing about."

"I like the development and behavioral classes better than this," Harper said.

"I do too, but for now, try to ease up on telling me I can just throw away something important."

Harper paused, as she had been forcing her way out of the conversation and towards the stairs until she heard Lane say that. She turned and looked at her. "Hey, I'm sorry. So what's this trip all about?"

Lane pressed her palms against the table. "I'm so glad you asked!"

That night, Lane found herself opening the pregnancy test on the tablet. She pushed her finger next to the scanner and set the tablet down as it ran the scanner and hormone diagnostics. Harper was reading next to her, much more calm and composed on the outside than she should have been for the circumstances.

They had just had sex, but neither felt like they were making love. The ardent breathing like they were in a wind race was truant. The glory of closing one's eyes and seeing only whiteness and light was unavailable to both of them. Even a modest saturation other than that given by the shower head was absent.

As they sat next to one another in bed, both wrapped in towels that were finding ways off of their bodies, they both remained quiet. Harper's eyes found ways to move from her book to give sidelong glances at Lane, continually putting words in her head that she would say, but withholding them at the last moment. Lane was fidgeting with the tablet, rolling up the edges of it and moving her finger about slowly and steadily as she found ways around opening up the testing app until, finally, she had done so and it was calculating. Only then, when the tablet was next to her and her fingers were still fidgeting did Harper say something.

"You seem nervous," she said.

Lane nodded grimly. "Yeah, it's this trip, the one to the mountains with the karate dojo. I guess—" She faltered to validate her excuse. There were few fears and the only ones she could think of related back to pregnancy. She wanted to remain hopeful, but if she brought that up now, Harper would ask her to test it and she would have to tell her it was processing. She wanted to hold back until she knew for certain.

"What about it?" Harper pried at her.

"My sensei's wife," Lane said. "I find her nettlesome."

"What has she said?"

"I don't know her all that well," she said.

Harper shook her head at Lane. "Then what about her is it?"

Lane reached. "The way she frowned when I asked if you could come to this trip."

"Well, if they don't want me to come—" Harper began.

"No, they do. They do. Well, at least my sensei does. He immediately liked the idea."

Harper set her book down. "I think it's time we talked"—starting the sentence like that gave them both hidden anxieties, but Harper pushed past them to keep talking—"about how neither of us get along with women very well."

"What? How could you—" Lane stopped herself, realizing, "there is a pattern there."

"Modus ponens," Harper sighed.

"What's that mean?" Lane asked.

"If I talk to a woman who isn't my wife, we'll begin arguing. I'm talking to a woman that isn't my wife, therefore we'll be arguing."

Lane squinted and her nose pushed towards her eyes. She asked, "What's that you're using?"

Harper said, "Modus ponens, which is a method of arguing with cause and effec putting things in perspective with patterns."

"That doesn't help us," Lane sighed, checking the tablet.

"It puts my mind at ease to recite things," Harper said idly.

Lane cocked her head and put her hand on Harper's shoulder. "What's getting you all worked up?"

"Your sensei's wife," Harper said as she realized she was very much afraid of putting too much pressure on Lane to have become pregnant. Not only was she counting on starting a family with Lane to have her retirement absolute, she knew she could have no more eggs taken from her to be fertilized with sperm. What she had already given her was the only chance the two of them had. Not only that, Harper thought, I didn't have the gall to even be there. I wanted to avoid blaming myself if it went wrong by excluding myself entirely.

Harper watched Lane check her tablet again and said, "I think modus tollens much more suiting tonight," she looked down to see Lane observing her. When their eyes met, Lane smiled widely and Harper inhaled., "I'm not arguing, therefore I must not be talking to a woman that is my wife."

Lane pulled her arm as she said. "You should teach classes at my college. You'd be so good at it."

"You just want me to stop bringing up old philosophical corpses in bed," Harper said, jest in her eyes. "Well, I've got news for you. I would talk even more about it in bed if I was doing it behind a desk all day." She touched her nose to Lane's and rubbed them together happily.

"I can tell you don't get to talk too much at work," Lane said innocently.

Harper was a little bit shocked, as she knew this was the most appropriate chance she had to bring it up, but there was a flurry of activity from the tablet as a ding reverberated from it. Lane lifted herself quickly and grabbed at the tablet, holding it in front of her face.

"Oh, Harper!" she exclaimed.

Harper regarded Lane worriedly. "What is it?"

Lane held the tablet at arm's length and fell backwards into Harper's lap. "Oh, my love!"

"Yes, hello." Harper stroked Lane's hair. "What is it?"

"Don't you know?" Lane said wholeheartedly. "I am plump, I am rotund, I am amply filled. It is conclusive that soon I will be an overweight, fleshy mass that is filled with yours and mine!"

Harper held Lane's head between her hands, looking down into her sparkling brown eyes. "You mean you're pregnant?"

Harper squeezed her eyes nearly shut as she smiled and they spoke in unison. "Do I ever!"

Harper's eyes widened. "Straight answer, pet."

"Yes, yes, a million times, yes." Lane's legs and arms shot from where she was laying and Harper's head rolled back on her neck as her hand held her forehead.

She began laughing emphatically. "Why I ought to—"

Lane wistfully said, "Shower me with compliments? Yes, you ought to do that."

"Oh, come here!" Harper lifted her legs from under Lane and jumped atop her, kissing her neck, then cheeks. Finally, the ardent breathing, the dousing, the ephemeral white light, all returned to the pair that night.

Chapter Twenty-Two

They met at the dojo, a place Harper had only been to once to see if it was somewhere she would like to be. It was still dark and the sky was slowly removing the drapery it had instilled, a pattern resembling the night sky. Pale blue gauze pushed at the boundaries of earth and sky as the sun delicately emerged from the eastern edge of the ocean.

When a dozen or so people were standing about in a semi-circle, kicking the rocks of the parking lot they had hurried past so many times on their way to class, Lane's sensei clapped his hands and smiled at them all, giving eye contact to each person individually as his hands remained pressed together.

"Hello, I am Sensei Jal." Harper tucked away a smile as she listened; there was something about his accent she found funny. "Nice to see some old faces," he said, "and to meet some of you for maybe the first time. Today and tomorrow we will be in what some consider the jungle. Up in those mountains we will practice some of our training, some of our combat skills, and a lot of technique. If you are not currently training at the dojo and are coming with us, I invite you to join in during everything. That's what you paid for, isn't it?"

Harper looked to Lane and Lane smiled out of the corner of her mouth, shrugging. Harper pushed her smile down to remain serious as she listened to Jal. "I hope we all have fun and, most importantly, stay safe." Harper put a hand on Lane's shoulder, rubbing her and reminding her with her touch why she should stay safe.

"If you don't, I'm always available, even if I don't want to be," came a voice from the crowd. A few parted to show a paunchy man smiling at them.

"Yes," Jal said, voice wavering, "we have a registered nurse coming with us. You may all know him as the green belt with the blocks of a brown belt, but I know him as John."

"Hi," said John.

Jal looked to the dim sky. "Let's actually go around the circle and introduce yourselves and say how much karate experience you have."

When it came to Harper, she said, "Harper Trill. I have so little experience that I don't even know how to pronounce karate."

"Karate," Jal said with a flourish on the e.

"See, I didn't know that," Harper said.

"It might just be my accent," Jal said, fixing her eyes carefully with his.

Harper's eyes smiled. "Might just be."

"Hi, I'm Lane, I have been coming to this dojo for a year now, but I took a lot of karate in my late teens and taught it to elementary school classes a bit in my twenties." A few students said some words of congratulations, having not known this, and Sensei Jal smiled at her, giving a look of significance for what she'd said.

At the end of the greetings, everyone found their ways to their cars and in a line like children holding hands as they crossed the road, they each followed the car in front of them through the city streets, then out of the city through one mountain pass until the road turned to white gravel and they were all driving rapidly to catch up to the lead car. The gravel road soon turned into one of broken, pale asphalt, then they turned off into a red dirt road.

The land fell into valleys of endless cane fields, a verdant mass that swept across the land, perturbed only by jutting, rounded mountains and pockets of houses, perhaps four clustered immediately against the other. They were the homes of the field workers, placed pragmatically to allow for the people that worked the fields to devote their efforts to that and only that. Long roads raised themselves out of the sides of every patch, embankments on either side with a level top surface. The man-made terrepleins were well worn and of red dirt, contrasting with the green of the cubicles of viridescent fields that drifted with the breeze like undulating waves of the ocean.

Lane watched the ducks, dogs, and cats roaming the long thoroughfares. The motorcade turned away from the bucolic scene and began up a mountain pass.

"See that?" Harper jutted her jaw towards the fleeting view below in a gulley. "Those are rice fields."

"I think it was cane," Lane said.

"No, those fields back there were cane fields, which are atrocious. Most places just burn the fields after the season. It adds this toxic smoke to the air and you have to wait three years to grow again. Sugar cane, it's disgusting," Harper told her.

"How can you tell so quickly?"

"Rice fields are wet. They're grown in about two feet of water. This takes me back." Harper smiled.

"Back to what?"

"I worked on a taro farm, which is grown just like rice. Some farmers like to grow taro dry, but it just isn't the same. Those wet fields are treacherous in some regions. Snakes like to live in them. Not only that, a lot of snail shells break in the mud and as you kneel or walk in the field you can cut yourself open."

"Doesn't sound so bad," Lane said.

Harper was getting choked up. "I had a friend die when he cut himself open and didn't care about the wound.

Thought he was a tough guy. Well, that mud is really dirty stuff to be going into your blood stream. We weren't close to a hospital and he died of a staph infection."

"Holy shoots," Lane muttered under her breath.

"Yeah, man. We thought we had completed this perfect mission, killed the bad guys, etcetera. Then that happened!"

"Why were you on the farm in the first place?" Lane asked incredulously.

Harper watched the road. "We finished before we were scheduled for airlift, so had to find a new place to stay, seeing as we had already done our dance and taken out the reigning lord of the area. Greasy guy. So we did a work-related trade to a neighboring farm. We couldn't really go boasting that we deserved their highest honors for what we had done, so we pretended to be lost travelers that needed food and a roof. I learned a lot in that month."

"You were there a month?"

"I was exceptionally good at my job," Harper smiled out the side of her mouth. She thought of the group she had with her, all exceptional men and women. A few had died or been wounded in combat. She thoughtfully held a breath for a man she had gotten to know named Tre whose shock had induced him to do some terrible things.

"How'd you kill him?" Lane asked excitedly.

Harper's face fell. "Classified."

"You don't want me to know."

"You're right, I don't."

Lane gripped Harper's arm across the car. "You want to tell me," she said.

"You're wrong. When did you do that?"

"Oh, it was before we went back to the desert and he got himself hurt, which was early 22's. So, likely Christmas Eve."

"And who were you dating at the time?" Lane asked behind a smiling facade.

"Oh, no one. After Cecilia, there was nobody."

"Cecilia?"

"Why, have I never told you about her? Wild one, really. You would have loved her," Harper said.

"Likely not." Lane pressed the back of her head against the seat. "Popping your—"

"Cut it out, we were in love."

"Youngins."

Harper laughed and then said, in a revelation, "I don't know about the first person you have loved."

There was a stillness that hung in the silence that only existed inside the car. Outside the car, pockets of lives they didn't live passed by the car at an alarming speed.

Only in the last century, and because of Einstein and Hubble, have humans revised what a moving Universe means and only in the last decade have humans been able to apply that same knowledge to the jurisdiction of their galaxy in that it, too, is decentralizing and expanding. And in that moment of quietude amongst lovers, Harper theorized it might happen on a smaller, human-sized level, too.

Harper did not breathe until after she had said, "And why is it so hard to talk about these things? I want you to know how to grow taro and then move into the jungle with me and never have to think about me killing men, ever."

There was both relief and hostility in her voice as Lane said, "Oh, so it's only men, eh?"

Harper sighed deeply, thinking of why she had never gotten the opportunity to study the art of lying to women as well. "Yes, pet, only men."

"How exciting! With big guns?"

Harper chuckled. "I don't need a gun, love." Her hushed, humble, yet confident way of laughing that off was disquieting to Lane and she continued to hold herself close to Harper, but remained quiet now as her eyes tracked the images from outside and her mind grew increasingly unsettled.

"Woh, now," Harper muttered as the Oldsmobile drew to a stop under her foot's pressure. She wiggled the stick, then pushed it into position as she realized nobody in front of her was moving.

"Ah, there are some goats in the road," Lane cooed.

"Want to go on a rescue mission?" Harper asked her, ready to jump out of the car and get them.

"No, Sensei's got it."

"Ah, you're right," Harper said as she watched Jal smile to the cars behind him and his students. He pushed his arm under the belly of one of the goats, then scooped up a second with his other arm. He waddled slowly, taking his time to ensure nothing went wrong before dispersing the goats on the other side of the road. He was repeating the process when the passenger door to his car opened and his wife tried to capture the last one on the road. He looked back, placed the two down, and ran towards the pair of running, bleating animals.

He put a hand on his wife's shoulder to stop her from chasing the last goat, which was leaping and rearing now, unable to be coaxed into her arms. With ease and grace, he approached the goat and it was in his arms before it had looked his way. He waved again before getting back in his car. The procession of cars behind him slowly shifted their motors and, once he had pushed forward past the bend in the road where the goats had been, they followed.

Harper smiled and looked to Lane as they began to drive again. "You really trust this guy, don't you?"

Lane looked at her, smiling conservatively. "Is that such a bad thing?"

Harper said, "Has a dead ancestor appeared in the sky to tell you not to?"

Lane laughed. "What? No, that sure hasn't happened."

"Then it can't be such a bad decision." Harper smiled as she spoke.

Lane smiled towards the window, watching the current of green sway, pushed and pulled by an invisible force. The jungle around them would at once grip them, creating a canopy and sheathing them completely, then open up and spit them into the sunny, open road. Their procession followed Jal's front car for miles and hours, until Lane was apathetically tracing her finger across the window pane, creating intricate patterns with the oils from her fingers.

"Oh, finally," she heard Harper say, and looked over to her, then up to the cars pulling to the side of the road. They were in the middle of the jungle. Ropes and vines lashed their way from tree branches to trunks, as buntings are lashed across doorways and halls. The trunks of trees, more than five men wide, pushed from the turf for many feet, nearly a hundred, before their boughs fully spread out. Lane let her head fall back on her shoulders and she looked up, circling around to view the massive growths around her. Harper got out, quickly finding herself jutting away from the languorous drive and feeling freed.

"We have quite a hike to our accommodations," Jal yelled to everyone as the majority were looking as awestruck as Lane.

Harper touched her back, having already gotten their bag, and said, "Come on."

Birds vociferated the group's arrival as they pushed into a small opening in the flora. There were a great many rustlings in the trees overhead as they found their footing. The path was laden with rocks and stones that made their footing nearly impossible.

Lane walked behind Harper, watching her wife's feet step rhythmically either up, left, or right, copying as nearly as she could to take the same path. The group seemed to draw in a breath as Jal rounded a bend and their path began to parallel that of a thrashing brown river.

"Looks dangerous," Lane muttered.

Jal did not seem to falter or pause to take in the watercourse and neither did they.

After a few minutes of walking next to it, Jal substantiated the claim by saying, "Quite a few giant tarpon and dogfish tuna in these waters."

His wife muttered, "Are you telling us not to fall in?" He turned during his step to smile at her.

Harper turned to smile at Lane, a happy way to protest any possible pain to befall her, saying, "Take note."

Grouping together, they found themselves conglomerating under a forest clearing. Because Jal stood in it, everyone else followed suit and did not push past it, deeper into the jungle, but spread out instead. Jal watched as everyone filed in, and then, hands on his hips, he beamed at them all and raised his arms.

"Beautiful place, isn't it?" he asked rhetorically. "Because of the old embargo, nobody came here for many years. Nobody could. It was immune to the current anthropocene age where ecosystems are substantially altered by humans.

"Only those living here and some, but not many, visited. The past ten years have been different, though, and the next ten years may change even more. We practice every day to defend ourselves, but the animals, plants, and water have not built up a way to defend against us." He smiled during his sad sermon. "So let's not cause any greater detriment to the place we are than we already have.

"That being said, I want you to partner up, and we'll practice here for a few minutes, now that we are warmed up. If you have brought your partner with you, partner with them and guide them along with us. Now, Michelle and I will demonstrate." Jal ushered his wife over. " She nodded and he pointed to her quickly. She nodded again and blocked his upper, middle, and lower punches with her forearms. He nodded quickly and they turned towards the group. "The more experienced student should begin with the blocks. Hajime."

"Okay, Harp, let's do this!" They both bowed and Lane nodded. Harper pushed her fist from her side, directing it at Lane's forehead. Lane blocked it and Harper pushed her left hand—this time towards Lane's chest, which was blocked, then belly. Her fist stopped short as she chose mid-strike to give a wide berth between her fist and Lane's body.

"Going easy on me?" Lane asked after she had blocked it.

Harper replied, "I don't want to impair the most important place on your body."

Lane laughed as they continued to punch and block, saying, "You mean baby-making factory?"

"Yeah, that's one way to talk about it," Harper said, rolling her eyes as she lunged forward to punch.

Jal walked next to Harper and touched her elbow with his hand. The impetus surprised her and she twisted out of his grasp.

"Harper—" Lane said.

"I was trying to show you that your elbow can be drawn even further back. Is that alright?" he asked calmly. Harper looked down, then back at him, and nodded. "Then if that's fine, I'd like to show how to pull your elbow back, like it's being pulled by a rubber band. Then, when you want to strike, that rubber band releases and you have much more power behind your punch."

"I guess I was getting lazy, and, uh... thanks."

"It's easy to not know for someone that is not trained."

"No—I, uh..." Harper's voice trailed off as he looked at her, inquiry in his eyes.

"Thank you, Sensei!" Lane said quickly and he smiled, tucked his hands behind his back, and moved on. After he was working with another pairing, she said, "he does that, it's helpful."

"I'll try to treat it as such," she said. "Does he do that often?"

"What?"

Harper sibilated, "Touch you?"

Lane smiled it off with disregard.

"Well?" she asked Lane.

"Yeah Harper, he does it all the time. It's not a problem for me." She thought quickly about telling her she could ask him to stop, but remembered the yoga instructor saying something in a similar vein and said, instead, "It's a little synonymous with weakness to be afraid of something so simple."

Harper gave him a sidelong glance. "It's not unusual for a man to die after he touches me, pet."

"Calm down," Lane hissed.

"I think that's enough," Jal said placidly from the front of the group. A few students gave small cheers and he said, "you're not tired, are you? We still have a bit of a hike, you know."

They followed him deeper into the jungle. Wet stains appeared on the shirts and pants of all but a few members. Lane watched Harper's back and saw the incidental tracks of sweat tumbling down her back and around her shoulders.

"Jal?" Harper found herself asking as they traversed a more open part of the trail.

He looked back as he walked. "Yes?"

"Are we going to a Cayo?" she asked.

He smiled and looked forward. "Don't tell me how you knew, but yes."

"What's that?" Lane asked her.

"A cove. He's taking us somewhere special."

Lane asked, "How did you know?"

"It's a big island, but it's not that big."

Lane poked Harper's ribs as they walked upwards, pushing into the hill. "I think you have a compass somewhere in there. Hey, speaking of which, the office won't be too upset to not have you available for a job?"

Harper looked at her frantically. "Lane, not here."

"What? It's just a question." Harper sighed and the exhalation contained complaints enough to stop the stirring of Lane's words. She blinked at her wife's formal face, set and rigid, lips protruding in a tight, sealed way. She looked away to see Michelle watching her with wide, blue eyes. They twinkled as she smiled and looked away. Harper looked down to see Lane grabbing for her hand and she stroked the soft area between Lane's thumb and forefinger.

Harper leaned near to Lane's shoulder and kissed her neck, whispering, "It's a question you should bring up again in private, pet."

"Okay," Lane said softly, eyes still trained on Michelle. She felt endangered.

They were led onto a sandy trail where old, almost derelict beach houses became visible to them.

Harper breathed out, "These are from before Castro's time."

"You're right," Jal said. "Some of them were converted into refuges for children suffering from radiation in his time. See, the Cuban government was happy to have them here and let them come and paid for their treatment. Then they were moved to an area inside Havana, until the embargo was lifted and the U.S. bought Cuba, then they were forced back here."

"You can't be serious," Harper said, ashamedly. "We did that?"

Jal shook his head. "No, you had nothing at all to do with it. It was tourism and the U.S. government that did it in 2030."

Lane looked at Harper with pity, but Harper shook her head and closed her eyes. "Let's go, then."

Jal pushed the group forward by walking and talking. "I have had the joy of sharing this beach with the children, as well as from a few others that own or rent, and I think it will be an ideal place to train for the weekend."

Harper looked around, dismayed. "Why does my past always have a way of catching up with me?"

"Were you even alive when Chernobyl broke down?" Lane asked her.

"That is not the point," she replied.

Lane forced a smile. "Exactly. You're in the clear on this one. Seriously, Harper, stop worrying. This is like a vacation. Except with exercise. A work vacation."

"Pet, it's fine. I'm fine. You can stop."

"Just trying to help," Lane said as they walked onward.

Harper pushed her face into Lane's brown hair and waved her nose around in it like a flag in the wind. "You are, you are."

"Now, we have three bungalows and twelve people," Jal said, clapping his hands together in front of his body. "Don't worry, they have four beds apiece. You know what that means." Harper looked at Lane, jaw jutting out.

Michelle walked towards the couple, waving and saying, "Hiya, Jal and I want to know if you'd share a bungalow."

Harper grasped her bottom lip in her mouth, looking to Lane, who said, "That sounds wonderful."

"Great, I'll let him know. We'll take the one closest to the beach. It has the very best view," she said as she turned and sprinted quickly away.

"That's great," Harper said, "Like we need that. To share a house with a hetero—"

Lane cut her off. "Harper, this was supposed to be fun for me."

Harper sighed. "It'll be fun for someone, all right."

"Get over your qualms," Lane muttered, "and get in there."

The bungalows were separated by verdant, overgrown flora that pushed at its barriers and plunged under their feet. The red brick houses were quaint, patched together and holding no excess. The tin roofs were antiquated but bore no holes nor needed reparations and Harper and Lane felt equally content once inside the far bungalow. They locked eyes as they entered, their smiles growing fast as they realized the place carried a strong resemblance to a vacation they had taken many years before.

"Is this like...?" Lane began to ask.

Harper finished where she had taken off. "Maui?"

"We had our honeymoon there, didn't we?"

Harper held a smile as she asked, "Oh, why couldn't we have just gone to a hotel?"

Lane laughed. "Because they were on the boring side of the island!"

"Well, we were on some farmer's land during the wet season, pet! It wasn't the pampered experience I was hoping to have on my honeymoon!" Harper put the bag inside one of the few rooms and looked at the two twin beds inside.

Lane followed her halfway into the room, then back out. She said, "It was natural that way. It would have felt so sterile and plain to me, otherwise."

Harper laughed. "We were on a farm there too, of course it was organic. Hey, that was a taro farm, by the way, Lane."

"What? Why didn't you tell me while we were there?" Lane asked innocently.

Harper's mind stumbled even before she could get words out. "Well, Iuh. I didn't want you knowing at the time."

"What's changed?" Lane asked, leading the conversation now.

Harper's emotions were becoming crowded in her utterances. "Well, now I feel that it is a good time to tell you —"

Thinking that that concluded Harper's pronouncement, Lane pointed out, "Weather's a lot better, here, isn't it?"

"Let's hope, or we'll have another sleepless night."

"Now that was nobody's fault," Lane said, her voice full of recognition as her eyebrows raised.

"You only say that because I was down on you for so lon —hello!"

Jal and Michelle had walked in the door and the women halted their discussion to turn to them. Harper's hand went to her neck, stroking the back of it anxiously and Lane grabbed at Harper's waist. They both smiled spontaneously.

"Hi, you two, enjoying the interior?" Jal asked.

"Oh, yes."

"Very much."

Michelle laughed. "Good. Well, John started a bonfire and since it's too late to train again tonight we thought we could all have a little get together there."

"Sounds good," they chimed together.

Harper looked down at Lane's waist, saying, "Yup," as she put other thoughts aside and followed her out of the bungalow.

The pale sand of the beach threw itself away from the green of the ensuing jungle as it gained purchase and then, abruptly, was halted by the serene azure water. Lane took Harper's hand in hers and they walked briskly away from the group of those concentrated around the fire until they were well enough away to not be heard or too well seen. They simultaneously began a more lead-footed path through the sand.

"What if everyone on earth was able to be with their love interest?" Harper asked Lane, her angular face softened by the query coming from her lips. "I know it's logically impossible, but what if everyone that is in love was able to be with that person?"

Lane shook her head. "I had a science teacher who thought like that."

"No, really. Everything would come to a standstill. Nobody would be out to prove anything anymore, they would stop rummaging around trying to prove their power. Everybody would be in bed all day."

"I like to think the idiot savants—people that are autistic —and truly intelligent people would not fall prey."

"You like to think being in love is a weakness, pet?"

Lane dismissed it, then said, "I don't like to see it as the only reason we do anything." The water lapped towards them and, without saying they would, they both walked closer to the harder, wet, packed sand where the tide was pursuing the beach.

"Well, I like to think that the world would nearly stop if everybody could just have requited love," Harper said.

"You're one of the people still doing things, though, and I love you just as you love me, right?"

Harper hesitated, thinking of her job, thinking of how to tell Lane, but Lane took the hesitation to mean something very different and she spoke over Harper's indecisiveness, avoiding some unknown humiliation by saying, "Love is a broken vase whose shape everyone remembers differently."

Harper was happy for the shift from the delicate topic. "Who said that?"

"Anis Mojgnai, a spoken word poet from a few decades ago. Let's go back now."

"Nice memory, Lane. Yes, let's."

The fire was crackling and calling to them from where the karate students were, some of which could be heard whispering questions about Harper as they approached. Jal remained placid, observing all with calm eyes. Michelle was more outspoken than Jal, her words coming off as effectual and constructive when she made them, much like Jal's. Tonight, in such a vague social situation, Lane thought she saw a different man, more reserved and capable of loosening his control of the people around him, unlike his presence in classes at the dojo.

A woman extended her hand as they sat down. "Hi, Mary. You're Harper, Lane's wife. What is it you do?"

"Me?" Harper put a hand on her chest. "I'm in re-allocation services."

Mary nodded her head slowly, muttering out, "Oh," before finding a new question. "And where are you from?"

Harper told her, "My family is from this very island, actually."

"Oh, how sweet. I just assumed you were African-American. Did your family work in the fields?" Mary said plainly. She cocked her head, expecting a response.

Harper looked away and Lane held her hand in hers, understanding, and forced a laugh. "It's funny. People think I am from another country, like China, even though my family has been here for 150 years. Tell me, how long have you lived here?"

"Since the embargo was lifted in 2030," Mary told them both.

Lane spoke to her as Harper looked away. "So, not a long time. How much white are you?"

"I beg your pardon?" Mary asked.

"Oh, it's just a question I get quite a bit," Harper said, her tone heavily laced with passivity. "I get asked how much black do I have in me. Lane wants to know how much white you have," Harper's cheeks were making a pointed effort towards her mouth to keep it closed, now that she had spoken. She said nothing more, counting to ten in her head, then counting beyond that to calm herself down.

Mary stumbled with words, then began speaking again, saying, "What did your parents do here, Harper?"

Harper ground her teeth, wondering if it was so hard to imagine the professions black women and men could take up in a country that was predominantly black at the time. Now, it was different. Now, they were misfits in a continually whitewashed country. "They were both dancers. It's how they met, actually."

The speaker gasped. "How interesting! John, she comes from a dance family."

The registered nurse, John, looked to them, disengaging from another conversation, and said, "Really? My daughter's been getting into Irish River Dance since about a month ago."

Harper genuinely smiled. "I love Irish River Dance. There's so much history behind it."

"Really?" John asked.

"Oh, yeah. Do you want to hear about it?" She was looking at John, but saw Mary pucker her lips and turn away in her peripherals. Harper's smile widened.

"Yeah, of course," John said.

"Well, the Irish were being highly oppressed and they were basically told to not have any fun. None. No fires, no laughing, and absolutely no dancing. No dancing. The trouble with the regulation was that is defined dancing for the Irish as any rhythmic dancing of the arms and legs."

John added, "And in river dancing they only stomp around."

Harper made a faux-disapproving face, her jaw jutting as she did and he laughed with her. "Sure, they 'stomp,' and were able to get around the regulation, but they weren't just doing it for fun. Think about the end of the dance, what usually happens?" John flailed his arms out, adding a slight movement to his fingers after a moment. Harper laughed out.

"Exactly. They use their arms. It was their own way of letting their oppressors know they were a strong people not willing to let their culture be stripped from them. To this day, the Irish are a pretty proud people." Lane was rubbing her back and Harper looked to her, asking, "did I say too much?"

Lane smiled, trusting John enough to hear her say, "I haven't seen you this animated about something in a while."

John nodded. "It's hard to get too excited with the world in the same sort of state. But, hey, at least the Krussian PM got it!"

"Oh," Harper said out loud, clutching her stomach.

"Did you hear about that?" John asked them both. "They're giving all kinds of stories, but I think we know what really happened."

Lane looked at her, having a significant idea but no explicit knowledge of what Harper knew. Her wife's adverse reaction was indicative enough for her to feel the demand to hasten the end of the discussion. Lane was torn between finding a cessation to Harper's hurt and understanding a detailed account of what it was Harper was hurt by. She made a quick decision. "It sounded terrible. I've heard all about it. No need for details, really, John."

"Hey, I'm in the field of knowing sick people. I can tell when someone doesn't need to hear about gore. We need soft people in this country. Too many with hearts of steel up in Washington, if you know what I mean."

"I do," Lane said quickly. "How old is your daughter?"

"Just turning eight," he told them.

"And she's not in karate?"

"No, she is, but she only goes maybe twice a week." John shrugged. "I want her to know how to protect herself."

"That's the thing I hear the most," Jal said. He was sitting down close to Lane. Lane's eyes flickered to the beer in his hand, which seemed out of place to her. An oddity to be held by such a strict purveyor of discipline and control. "Would you like one?" He held one to her and she shied from it, but tapped Harper's shoulder.

"I'll have hers, thank you," Harper said reflexively, not quite knowing what to do before realizing there was no problem in telling him. She looked at Lane and she shrugged, thinking the same thing.

"Ah, I forgot that we're toning down your training because of the baby on its way. Of course, you don't want to drink," Jal said. "What about you, Harper? Have you ever given training with us a thought?"

Harper shifted under the strain of the new impetus. "I have not, no."

"Maybe it would be something you could try."

"Maybe while we're here, yes?" she asked, mildly perturbed. She pulled from the beer bottle and let the carbonation from the beer tickle her gums and coat her throat as she swallowed.

Jal smiled. "We'll get a chance to see tomorrow."

"Won't we?" Harper said quickly.

He replied without ceasing to smile. "I hope."

"Then I hope we can, too."

Lane, sensing a battle of wills, forced herself to enter their conversation, saying, "Jal trained in Okinawa. Weren't you there for a time, Harper?"

Harper's jaw projected., "Doing what, Lane?"

Lane fumbled with words, then settled with, "Were you?"

"Sounds interesting, whatever it was," Jal said with a smile.

"It does, even to me, sound interesting because I was never there. I haven't been to Japan. Lane must have herself confused."

Lane swallowed. "Yes, I must."

Harper put the back of her hand to her cheek, trying to feign a sudden bout of tiredness. "Would you excuse me?"

"But of course," Jal said.

Lane followed her back to the bungalow and undressed with her.

"Sorry about that, Lane, I had to get away."

"No, I felt it, too."

Harper smiled as she smoothed out the sheets, then got in. "Good."

"Listen, Harp, there's something I've kept from you for a really long time."

Harper's eyes grew hard. "What is it? Come here, lay down."

Lane moved towards the bed. "This email came for me to go to a memorial. For a woman I dated. A long time ago, but still." Lane breathed in sharply, clasping in her bottom lip and asked, "have you ever hurt someone?"

"Do you want me to answer or do you want me to tell you my stories?" Harper said. "I have a lot on that particular subject."

Lane shook her head and spoke. "She killed herself after we broke up."

"That's not true, then," Harper said, leaning her head closer to Lane's as she swept hairs away from her face.

Lane's head fell back down. "Oh yes, it is."

"No, it's not true that you hurt her. She hurt herself."

Lane looked to Harper with tears curving from her eyelids to her eyes, barely in place and broiling in the small container before falling. "Didn't I?"

Harper looked at Lane and relinquished any right to comment with her prolonged silence. Harper thought of the cuts on her own arms and what she hadn't told Lane. She resolved to tell her, not now, not while Lane was unearthing such old and traumatic memories, but she would.

"She was studying and working constantly," Lane interjected quickly, into the silence, an appeasing tone betraying her guilt, like she was trying to speak directly to Ashna. Her lips continued as she heard the words that she had once knew well. well come out of her, "She was always so smart. She had studied a lot as a kid. Well, after we broke up, she ran away for a few months then got herself killed in a river, somehow. It seemed like a suicide, but who knows. It really shook me."

"Why are we afraid to tell one another these things?" Harper asked, eyes and cheeks wet.

Lane licked the tear streaming next to the corner of her mouth and spoke quietly, "If I move past things in my past, will I move past my marriage?"

Harper's eyes pushed together., "I hope not."

Lane nearly laughed as she said, "Me too."

Harper grabbed Lane's waist and moved closer to her, whispering, "The past is where the worst things to have happened to us."

Lane looked at her, a wry smile drawn across her face, then turned away and sighed., "I think so, too."

Harper continued, "If you ever battle yourself, the war will be won only when you die."

"Never have been a fighter, myself."

Harper laughed., "Well, you know me."

Lane turned, shifting her tired body to look at Harper as she said, "Don't think I do. Hi, Harper, nice to meet you. Special operative for the government, is that what you said you did?"

Harper laughed and stroked Lane's long hair, her black eyes catching the pale moonlight as Lane's breathing slowed and she became thoughtless in sleep.

Harper knew there was no danger in the places she had avoided for so long, except in the monotony. The light of the night caught the pooling of tears in her eyes as fear caught in her throat immediately before she pushed a hand against her face and turned to lay down.

Chapter Twenty-Three

The morning tide swept away as the sun swept in, its sharp, diligent rays finding every place of murk and uplifting them all in a warm equity. The women stirred frequently in its glow, Harper being the first to begin to disentangle from their conjoined bodies and to push herself from the minute twin bed. Lane looked up to her, then shrugged her shoulders up until she found her hands were next to her breasts and were pushing off from the bed.

Harper smiled delicately as she cupped her hand under Lane's chin, then slipped off her soft pants and put on a pair or spandex shorts and a tank top. Lane grabbed for her workout clothes, much simpler and less formal than the gi she was used to wearing for karate training. Something about preparing for karate in such a different way struck her as impious. She sat on the edge of the bed, holding the clothes in one hand, balled up, and cupping her chin in the other.

"You okay, pet?"

Lane nodded slowly. "Yeah, it just feels weird getting to train without putting on a gi, driving to the dojo, all of that."

"It's not weird because I'm here?"

"That's an easier explanation," Harper said.

"Is it?" Harper asked. "It seems more difficult to think that." I'll meet you outside, how about that?"

Lane nodded softly. As she splashed her face in the kitchen sink with cold water, Harper was jogging quickly to the group on the beach. Michelle was leading them in warming up. Hands on her hips, Harper moved her feet in and out, then up and down. She leaned into lunges and began to feel the comfort of her blood warming inside her.

"Hey," Lane said as she stood next to Harper, catching herself up on the exercises.

After a few moments, Jal stepped in. "Let's begin by spreading out and beginning our katas. It is a truly unique experience to do a kata on the beach because you're able to see the path that you've taken in the sand, like a text you're reading from history. Let's start with our first kata."

Harper asked Lane, "Does he make up his own katas?"

Lane whispered back during her bow, "He hasn't mentioned it. Ask him?"

Harper realized she would rather not and watched Lane, as if she was following along from watching her body's movements.

"You are really fluid," Harper told her.

Lane was caught between telling her it was impolite to talk and thanking her, so opted for the latter. "Thanks. I can't tell if you are."

"I'm getting by."

Jal had them begin the next kata, coming over to Lane and pushing her down into the stance. He stood next to Harper, watching her move for the duration of the kata. Without any other commands or questions, he said, "Next one." The group began the next karate dance and he watched Harper closely, still. She saw him in her peripherals, but her eyes were trained on Lane's body. She scanned her wife's movement before she made hers, careful not to act too quickly.

When they were finished, Jal looked away from her and took two steps in the sand away, then turned back to tell everyone, "Today, everyone does every kata. All the way up to the black belt katas. If you don't know what you're doing, follow those around you. If they don't know what they're doing, sit down."

Feeling garrulous now, Lane said giddily, "I've been looking them up on the tablet and memorizing them, even the ones he hasn't—" Lane turned to look at Harper, but realized her sensei was very near, listening. "—oh, hello."

He eyed them, asked everyone to bow, and started the count for the kata. Lane's form was not perfect, and Harper had trouble making the same mistakes as her, but she forced herself to. She detached herself from anything she had known before. She visualized a trash can, a great large one that the dump trucks pierce on both sides, and put into it every piece of training she had ever received, thinking only of what was in front of her.

Lane looked to Harper, sweat springing across her forehead in the pale morning sun. Her breath came from her without force and she opened her mouth to breathe from it and, when that failed, closed it to breathe from her nose. Her eyes vacillated as she looked at Harper, the look in them gaunt and grim.

"Sit down." Harper imposed her words on Lane and she nodded. She was torn between helping her and following her trained instincts to keep working.

Harper had not changed from the position of the kata she was on and Jal counted for the next one. She complied, her hand turning from a balled fist at her side to a knife striking the air behind her as she brought her right foot back and changed stances.

She gasped as she realized what she had done, how she had moved without watching Lane first. She closed her hand into a fist, turned it next to her groin, bowed, and sat down.

Harper felt an abject worry, but did not turn to Jal to begin groveling or dissembling, but looked to Lane. "Are you seeing black, yellow, tunnel-vision?"

"No, not anymore," she said softly. The smile she gave her looked genuine, but bleak.

The kata finished shortly and Jal clapped loudly, asking, "Does everyone here know how to swim? No, Susie? Well, everyone else, in the water. Susie, I'd like you to practice the first and second katas on the beach and give yourself a break when need be." He bent down to Lane. "Are you feeling okay?"

"Yes," she replied softly.

"Would it help to go into the ocean?"

Lane nodded happily, then sprung to her feet and walked away. Harper followed her, happy to see her feeling better than she had a moment ago. She felt she was in the custody of someone else and she twisted her body to see Jal watching her as Michelle approached him. The sensei's wife put a hand on his shoulder and started talking to him. He looked away from Harper to her, talking into her ear. Harper caught up to Lane and realized they were some of the first to jump into the water in their workout clothes.

"Everyone else is going up to get changed," Lane told her.

"I noticed, but I can stand to let these dry on the beach during another one of his grueling workouts," Harper said. "Are they all like that?"

"Oh, no. He never just stands in one place like that, going on and on with the same thing. I mean, they were different katas, but thirty minutes of the entire class doing them is sort of unordinary."

"You feel like a friendly ocean race?" Harper asked as they had finished wading in and were preparing to dive under.

Lane smiled. She had a very slight fear of the ocean, which Harper had worked at chipping away for years. The affable competition had been observed to construct something to take Lane's mind off of the distress she had a habit of building. They dove together into a lapping blue wave as it churned towards them. Lane popped up, immediately breathless, and turned her shoulder to whip her right arm backwards, then towards her head. As it hit the water, her other arm was reaching up behind her and propelling forwards in the air until it was submerged again. She let the new windmill-like rhythm dictate her thoughts as Harper's head sprung from the surface of the water near her. She laughed casually as her hand touched the top of her head, noticing the harm the water did to her hair. She pushed through the water in a frog-like fashion, forcing a laugh out of her own mouth as she did so.

The land became a soft ribbon of green and white when they had finished. Harper knew they were ready for a break when she was consistently keeping a ten to twenty foot gap between Lane and herself. She hung back and when Lane approached, she dove under the water, touching her ankles as she did.

"I knew it was you," Lane told her.

Harper laughed, squinting her eyes through the salt and sun pushing into them. "I wanted you to. I'm not out to scare you."

"Harper, I'm tired," Lane told her.

"I know you are, pet. Do some egg beaters to keep yourself floating." Lane complied and Harper watched the way the water was moving back and forth from the land of the cove. When Lane waded towards her and held onto one of her shoulders, Harper stroked her wet orb of hair. "Here, see where my hands point." Lane watched Harper's hand. "I'm going to let you in on the current events. Go back with me on that current, but notice that there are rip-currents coming back out to sea to either side of it. But it'll be really fast, and see how quickly it turns into waves that go towards the beach? Those will take you back to the beach fastest. "

"Hey, Harper," Lane said in a compressed voice.

"Yeah, pet?"

"I just wanted to say sorry for telling the sensei about you going to Japan."

"Oh, you mean Jal. No, not at all. You're not used to being on missions with me. Anyway, I'm done with all of that."

"What?" Harper saw Lane's eyes widen and her hand drew up from the water to shade her eyes.

"I'm on retirement leave, now." Harper finished her statement quickly. "All done."

Lane was pushing up further from the water, her legs kicking quickly as she spoke. "Do you know what this means for us?"

Harper nodded, lips jutting as she moved her jaw around, squirming her face from one smile to another. "I think I have a faint idea."

"Oh, Harp!" Lane kicked from the water and splashed into Harper, hugging her fully, cheek pressed into the back of her head and arms wrapped around her so much that she was holding her own shoulder as well.

"Careful, now, pet," Harper said as she broke the surface of the water with her hands and splashed furiously to keep them both afloat.

Lane held her back. "Why didn't you tell me?"

"No good time, I guess," Harper said.

Lane grew stern, saying, "Bad excuse," but it quickly dissolved. "Oh, I'm so happy!"

They swam back inland together, Lane clutching Harper's hand at one point as her fear returned to her during a particularly cold bit of ocean. Harper held her on her back and swam slowly for a time before they began to feel the push of waves bringing them back to the beach.

Harper felt an unease seeping from the shore before she had stopped swimming. She delicately let Lane slip off of her back and she surveyed the area, but only saw the group, under loose direction, sparring with one another.

Harper put a hand to her forehead, shielding her eyes from the glare from the white sand beach as she gazed towards it, asking, "Want to walk around the beach?"

Lane found her footing along the sandy bottom of the shore and said, "It couldn't hurt."

They walked up and then along the forest's edge, where it met dirt and pebbles and fell towards the sand of the beach. The plants crescendoed upwards on both sides of a valley to their left, a flowing and fluttering tropic wilderness. They caught themselves staring at the riveting landscape and were both caught off their guard when a young girl approached them.

"Hello," Harper said, looking down at the pale child.

Lane bent at the knees, becoming on the same eye-level as the nubile girl. "Where are you from?"

"Krussia," said the girl.

Harper's eyes alighted, staring at her wondrously, finding Krussia to be a place that she had continual problems forcing into an obsolete recess of her mind. Her ability to create facades was all but gone and her face was grim as she looked down at the anemic girl.

"Oh?" Lane asked her. "What are you doing here?"

"We come here," she answered simply.

"But why?" Harper asked.

Lane remembered and spoke for the girl. "To receive treatment for radiation contamination, right?"

"Yes," the girl said meekly, but with a slight propulsion that betrayed a memorization of her words. "Even forty years later we are still suffering from it."

"Do you like it here?" Lane asked, her voice syrupy and candied.

The girl batted her eyelids and spoke with unhindered esteem. "It is a paradise. Of course I love it here!"

Harper asked demurely, "Have you received the treatments?"

"Four years now, I have. My eyelashes have even begun to grow back." It was true, though the sun sparkled on her pale, hairless head, her blonde lashes blinked over her pale eyes.

"I am Lane," she said, then pointed to Harper, "and this is my wife, Harper."

Harper extended her hand, but the girl looked at it softly and smiled. "I am Nikola."

"Really? I mean, I met a man named Nikolav recently," Harper said quickly.

The girl was hopeful as she said, "Did you? I have a brother in Krussia named Nikolav. Were you there? Was it him?"

Harper's eyes flickered, then she said, "I hope not."

Lane looked to her, blinking as she looked at Harper's silhouette against the sun. Years ago, she had found adoration could quickly turn into a yearning to be adored. As she wondered about Harper and who she was with now, she wondered how she felt about herself as she stopped adoring that which adored her. Her eyes were still trained on Harper, watching her move and sway in the depths of her mind as she remained still and immobile in front of her eyes.

Harper shrugged. "It is the product of my past, Lane."

Lane's head quivered as she was brought out of her reverie by Harper's discerning ability to see into her shocked expression. "What's going on?" Harper asked, adding, "that never did upset you before, pet."

"Well, I hope you get better soon," Lane said to the girl in front of them.

Nikola smiled as theirs waned. "Oh, but I am better."

"You are, yes. You are," Lane said reservedly.

"Do you want to build a sand castle?" the girl Nikola asked.

Lane gave a giggle. "Would we ever?"

As they walked closer to the water's edge, Lane looked to Harper with downcast eyes. Harper articulated, "No part of the process is effectual unless the product is presented."

"I don't think I want to know one story about what you have done in full, because then I would need to hear every story."

"I'm willing to tell you every story, pet."

"Well, I'm not willing to hear them yet. They seem so disturbing, just by the tone you get when you hint at them."

"Well. I shouldn't be telling you anyway, because they're still—"

"Yeah," Lane cut her off, "confidential."

"Well," Harper said, "wars were ended because of me."

They sat on the brown sand with Nikola between them. Harper used her forearms to push the sand into a mound and Lane began shaping it as Nikola dug a trench.

"Have you ever seen this?" Harper asked as she dripped waterlogged sand onto the castle.

"A drip castle," Lane said.

Nikola nodded and repeated the technique many times. Relaxing, Lane and Harper leaned back on their palms then moved their faces to soak in the sun.

"You know, it is always so hard to get the tops right on normal castles, but with drip castles it is always so beautiful and delicate," Lane said.

Nikola nodded, her neck seemingly incapable of stopping as she moved her arms up and down to create new spires. Her mouth moved as she went through the travails of creation. As with many, her tongue became inevitably lodged between her lips, lolling out of her mouth as she became exceedingly focused on her task.

"Do you live here with your parents?" Harper asked.

"No," she said simply.

"Oh."

"I love it here, though."

"I would, too." Harper amended her statement. "I do."

Nikola spoke as she worked, never taking her eyes from the castle. "Many girls, they come here wearing wigs and are very self-conscious, but it is so beautiful and happy that they forget you are to be concerned with those things."

Harper did not know what put her in two separate worlds with the child, but the feeling was present and hindering.

Lane gave a laugh, "It's strange that we forget our original purpose as humans is to exchange information."

Harper looked at her, but remained bereft of the capacity for articulating herself. There was a descending sense of certainty that she was passively feeling within herself. She had no motivation to stimulate it with words that could potentially intensify her declivity.

Lane smiled at her, taking her silence to mean attentiveness to her words and spoke again. "We exchange love like it has a price, but it doesn't do any good to feel that way. The depreciation of love cheapens actual relationships."

Harper looked to her steadily and unshaken, like she would look at a reliable bird that remained in her frame of vision. If Lane were to fly like a bird out of Harper's line of vision, she would likely continue gazing in the same place that Lane had been.

The child broke them both of their preoccupations as she giggled a scream, pointing towards Harper. Moving her head towards the girl, she chewed her cheek with her molars and raised her eyebrows.

"The tide," Lane managed.

Without having time to move, Harper was hit by a wave at her back. "Ooof!" It was a warm water that soaked her back and rolled down her spine. It rushed around her thighs to grip her skin and soak into the shorts she wore.

Nikola giggled and asked, "Is it wet?"

"Yes, very," Harper said as she looked up at the two of them from a distance. They had jumped up and run backwards as they watched the wave consume her.

"I want to go in," the girl said.

"Are you allowed?" Lane asked, bending down to ask her.

"I want to go in, too." Harper nodded.

Lane looked around the beach, seeing a group of children of all ages, but all with similar appearances to Nikola's. She said, "Let's go towards your friends and swim over there."

"That is good," Nikola said, skipping ahead of them, then sprinting forward. Before Harper and Lane were ten feet from the sandcastle, Nikola was already splashing a child she knew and checking in with a supervisor.

Absently, Harper said, "Sick girl."

"When you're referring to someone, say who they are before anything else about them. She's a girl that's sick."

Harper nodded. "Absolutely, I shouldn't have to be schooled on something like that. That girl got pretty sick, which just makes me so worried about her. You're right, though, saying she's sick before saying she's a person isn't person-first language."

Lane's big toe skimmed the sand and Harper caught her elbow to ease her away from falling. "Thanks, Harper."

"For you, anything," Harper said as she wrapped her arms around Lane's shoulders and walked on.

"Hey, you okay?" Lane asked with innocence lacing her tone.

Harper looked at her, pushing a bleak smile onto her face. "Yeah, I am."

"You're not overcome with the desire to adopt this girl or something?" Lane asked, half-jesting.

"What? No." Harper smiled and poked Lane's belly gently. "Besides, we've got this."

Lane was calm as she said, "You don't mind not being able to take tests out here to make sure it's in there?"

Harper held her bottom lip between her teeth and shook her head. "No, I don't. I think you're doing a good job of safekeeping."

"Maybe it's not working that's getting me down," Harper said as they sat down to watch the children play.

"What about it? Do you want to be doing something more with your life?" Lane asked.

"It's not that I want to be doing something," Harper said, "I don't want the world-saving aspect of my job in my life, but I want the world to have me saving it, I guess."

Lane twirled her hand in the sand, unearthing a dark pattern amidst the pale top layer of sand, and said, "Living as if the world will not move without you tomorrow means your tomorrow will be very bleak if the world does not move for you."

Harper remained silent, but internally, she was invigorated by Lane's realism.

Lane pushed Harper's shoulder with her own. "Besides, you're a warrior, not a worrier. If you need to go change the world, don't think about it for the next forty years. Go, do it."

"You're sweet, pet, but I think I'm happy to stop all of that. I'm content to be a worrier. It means I'll have more opportunities to watch what the world does without me pushing it around, you know?"

Lane shut her eyes against the sun and said, "I believe I do. You know there's danger in the places you haven't gone, but never monotony."

"Let's swim out a little bit and join your karate buddies again, pet."

Lane nodded and they raced towards the crashing ocean waves. The frothy white dissipated into pale blue, then azure, then darker and darker hues the further from the water's edge they got. Harper's body dipped under the water and she twirled and glided, propelling herself with quick, swift movements. Lane's head bobbed in the water, switching sides as she threw large arm strokes through the water. Harper's eyes blinked in the water, straining to find the salty saturation comfortable, but she loved to see as far into the blue as she could. She watched the vast sway and churning as it appeared to her, a tiny and unfathomably unimportant aspect of it.

They swam back to shore, each of them holding their own weight this time as they pursued the seashore. They found their footing and abandoned the swim to pursue the circle of those practicing karate on the beach.

"Because Lane shouldn't spar and I don't know your skill level, Harper," Jal said as Harper and Lane walked towards the group, hand in hand, "I think we should spar."

Harper did not know she would feel flustered at such a request, and she only managed to say, "Oh?"

"Perhaps we can see a better gauge of your skill, this way," he said.

In some way, Harper felt it erroneous to try to exhibit any skill, but declining would divulge more than she was willing to.

She felt the irrevocability of the nod she gave Jal, then followed it up by saying, "Yes, that sounds quite nice. Should we do it here?"

"No," Jal said quickly, "the ground is less loose further up the beach." To showcase the vulnerability of the ground, he lightly kicked it.

"That sounds nice," Harper said as she walked up the beach with him, past loose black pebbles, and onto the flat, dark dirt of a small parcel free of vegetation.

Michelle and Lane were walking distantly behind and seemed to want to oversee. When both Jal and Harper were standing opposite of one another, they made to bow but Michelle's words were quicker than them and she said, "Rei."

Only then did Jal fully bow and Harper followed. "Do you want full contact, Jal?" Michelle asked. His eyebrows went up as he looked at Harper and she nodded curtly.

He said, "Hai."

"Full contact, then." Michelle added., "Be safe. Hajime."

As she said the latter word, Jal began bouncing on the balls of his feet, springing forward then, almost as quickly, bouncing backwards again. Harper's jaw jutted forward and she took a few light steps, noticing his technique and mirroring it at a lesser degree. She was not one to draw out the beginning of a fight and, instinctually, moved in for a head level punch, then a back fist when he blocked her punch.

He was surprised, only slightly, by the back fist and moved quickly to block it, but it was not where Harper was truly threatening. As he moved his block upwards, she struck a hip-level punch that would have made contact if he had not pushed backwards from the hip and dodged it.

Without letting him regain his footing, Harper moved her front left foot to the right, pivoting off of it to spin all the way around until her right leg was extending and she was making lost territory with a spinning back kick. She whipped her head like a ballerina's to not lose sight of him and she watched him barely step back and use the little time he had to react to put up his forearms in an attempt to block.

She did not let her leg extend all the way back, but worked her leg like a door on hinges and straightened it, then brought it back to his body, straightening it again as he re-adjusted his block, then opening it on him again and again. His defense weakened, but she was standing on only one foot and had to recover before he grabbed her kicking foot as it slowed. As she landed, she twisted another backhand towards his head and he jumped back, completely out of her range.

He bounced on the balls of his feet and Harper brought her hands up to block like a boxer's. She began faking to the left, doing it twice, then to the right once. She had gained area on him without letting him breathe. She watched him begin to bounce, shifting to the side and likely beginning to make a circle around her.

She stopped him with a roundhouse kick, which rarely made contact, though it was powerful if it did. It stopped him from bouncing around. Instead of bringing her right foot back when she landed the kick with it, she placed it squarely in the middle of his legs and began punching twice with her left hand, then once with the right. She did that pattern of punches a few time before she decided he would catch on, then alternated the pattern. He held his hands over his head, protecting himself, but also storing energy, she knew. He was half-watching her and she decided to try something that could hurt if he wasn't in control.

She extended both of her hands and put them over his hands, gripping them both and pushing them down. They nearly knocked against his forehead and his head was pushed downward as she brought her left knee up, quickly ascending it towards his face. She waited to see what he would do and he, almost immediately, had taken his right foot and brought it above her left leg, sweeping it right and removing her most stable balance point. He brought his leg up again and swept her right foot from under her. She gripped his hands and brought him with her.

He ducked, rolling on the ground with only his shoulders and she rolled with him. Her mouth caught sand and silt but her eyelashes deflected anything as she watched their movement and struck the ground with her heel and rounded her body over his. He was laying prone for only a moment, her hands on either side of his shoulder as she began to hitch her hips up to bring her knees to either side of his chest.

As she gained purchase on his body, he knocked one of her arms away from her body and as that side of her body dipped at the shoulder he regained a grip on her elbow and pulled her towards him as he pushed up at her with his hips. She fell, her face narrowly avoiding his as he pulled her even closer to the ground and swept her body around. He was nearly atop her, switching her legs around mid-air so, as they landed, she was laying beneath him.

Using the same technique he had, she thrust her hips and his body pushed forward. His fingers spread as his palms tried to make contact with the ground above her head, but she reached back, blindly, and grabbed his wrists before he could press his hands into the dirt and gain traction there. She pulled them out from under him and, to avoid his head hitting the ground he sprung from his feet and she was free of his pressure on her body, but she held onto his strong right arm as he moved upwards and wrapped her thigh behind his back and over his shoulder.

Her shin held onto his neck and the rest of her body followed until her other shin was wrapping around his neck just as he stood fully. His hands went up to her, but she was already swinging her torso. Her head and legs followed, spinning on either side of his body until the propulsion forced him off of his feet.

Harper opened her clasp on his neck and pushed her heels down to land on the ground as his body tumbled in the air. She watched it fall and watched as Michelle ran towards him.

"I think that's enough!" came Michelle's strong voice as the two combatants looked at one another.

Jal put a hand out and pressed against the dirt to stand. "Is it?" he asked her.

Harper's breath came heavy and she laughed her words out. "Not nearly."

Jal looked to Michelle and Harper to Lane. Both women were standing with open mouths, then, as the fighting duo looked to them, they stood up straighter and closed their mouths in unison, nodding.

Michelle's voice came louder, "Hajime."

Harper looked to the sun and put herself between it and Jal. She was just a silhouette to him now, and she kept her fists close to her body, punching them towards his body while he couldn't see her except in outline. He was perfectly illuminated to her and she saw his blocks perfectly, finding two openings to strike and taking advantage of both. He nearly doubled over then, as if he realized the asset that her position gave her. He sprung to the side, making a path to put himself between the sun and Harper.

She bent at her knees and dropped to her hands. A trail of sweat formed into her eye, forcing her to shake her head and squint. Without letting that perturb her, she squatted and thrust her leg from under her. Jal had to react quickly to avoid having his legs swept out from under him. His knees sprang to his chest and Harper realized he was going to land in the perfect position. From the ground, she ducked her shoulder and sprung from her feet, rolling under his body just before his feet landed.

He turned to face her as she ducked her head, catching his hip between her neck and shoulder. She pulled his body as he began to push it forward, towards her, and flipped him onto his back. His legs retracted towards his chest and he pushed them back towards the ground, jumping up after having been laid on his back. He swung his leg left to right, making contact with her shoulder and pushing her towards the ground. She gripped her knee and recovered as he pushed towards her, in a cat-stance and with his hands on a level plane in front of him. He pushed her body.

Without an obvious place on his body to pull, push, or punch, she fell meekly. She pushed up from her hands and, with one leg, swept across the ground where he stood again. He jumped, as he had before, to avoid being struck and she placed the foot that had been sweeping against the ground, shoving it into the dirt and sprung from its impetus to stand and block his flurry of punches. She waited, then, finding the pattern he was using, was able to expect a punch and, instead of blocking it away, she grabbed it and both twisted and hauled it towards her. She moved her head, then body to the side as she pulled his body away from its original position and far from her. He landed on the ground behind her.

His hand tapped the dirt three times and Harper took a few steps backwards, preparing to bow, then rushed forwards, along with Michelle.

"Jal?" Michelle asked.

Harper was breathless, but asked, "You okay?"

His smile could be seen, although his nose and mouth were pressed into the dirt. "You gave me a very good time, today, Harper. Thank you." His hand extended from under his chest and, with limited mobility between body and ground, he shook Harper's hand.

Michelle's jaw moved rigidly, then she said, "Kiotske." Jal and Harper complied, standing up. They faced each other, reconciling as they smiled wide and stood straighter than they had when they had begun. Michelle said, "Rei," and they both bowed. After they had finished the bow, they walked towards one another and shook hands. As she finished the handshake, Lane ran up to Harper and threw her hands around her head, kissing her cheek and wiping the grime from her shoulder.

"Thanks, pet."

"Thank you!" Lane said as she kissed Harper again. "You did so well, I'll never forget that."

"It's not about doing well," Jal told her, "it's about opening up the warrior's path in one another."

"Right," Lane said loudly, then whispered, "it's all about the lesson with this guy," into Harper's ear. Then, loudly, she said, "you were great!"

Harper laughed and said, "Perfect something and you'll have something to do. Do it for others and you'll have something to be proud of."

"Do you ever think of doing martial arts as a job?" Michelle asked her.

"I don't need to do anything as a job anymore."

"But don't you want the world to praise your efforts in it?" Lane asked her, gripping her arm.

Harper shrugged. "Loving requires you forget the world praises the individual, and find solitude in the praises of an individual." she touched Lane's nose. "That's you."

"What do you say we wash off?" Jal asked.

Harper nodded.

She was not happy to have dried off from the ocean only to be covered in sweat and red dirt, but she ran towards the water with the three of them anyway. Her hand clasped Lane's and they dragged their legs with a new strength, ripping lines in the water. Harper looked to Jal, who was bent over the water, splashing Michelle as she laughed, putting her forearms in front of her face to defend against the onslaught of water. Lane laughed as she tackled Harper at the waist, bringing her down and into the water. The crashing waves spun their bodies, separating them and forcing them to collide against the sand.

Breathing, relieved to have been forced above the water, Harper saw Lane's body in the water and jumped over her, pulling at her shoulders to drag her under water. Lane spun around to face her in the water, then, seeing it was Harper attacking her, she kicked her feet and pushed against her body. They rose from the water holding one another.

Murray yelled out, "Here they come!"

"Hey, guys!" called John, grabbing another karate member's hand and lumbering towards them.

Mary shouted, "Get the senseis!"

Harper and Lane clued in to their bellows and ran towards Michelle and Jal, tugging and pushing at the water to splash their faces. John used his arm to splash them and Mary kicked with her feet. Lane and Harper caught one another's eyes as they smiled, kissing one another's mouths as the smiles remained on their lips.